THE
THE WORLD'S

Folk Tales of Scotland

Norah and William
Montgomerie

Illustrated by
Norah Montgomerie

CENTRAL REGIONAL SCHOOL LIBRARY SERVICE F

CANONGATE · KELPIES

First published 1956 by The Hogarth Press Ltd, London
First published in Kelpies 1985

Copyright © William and Norah Montgomerie 1956

Cover illustration by Jill Downie

Printed in Great Britain
by Cox & Wyman Ltd, Reading, Berkshire

ISBN 0 86241 093 2

*The publishers acknowledge the financial assistance
of the Scottish Arts Council in the
publication of this volume*

We wish to acknowledge our indebtedness to the works of
Robert Chambers (1841), J. F. Campbell (1860),
John G. Campbell (1891), and Traill Dennison (1894)

Copy No. 5

Class No. 398.2

Author MON

CANONGATE PUBLISHING LTD
17 JEFFREY STREET, EDINBURGH EH1 1DR

CONTENTS

Introduction	page ix
The Well at the World's End	1
The Wee Bannock	5
Rashie Coat	9
The Flea and the Louse	13
Whuppity Stoorie	16
The Winning of Hyn-Hallow	20
The Maiden Fair and the Fountain Fairy	23
The Tale of the Soldier	29
Pippety Pew	34
The Black Bull of Norroway	38
The Last of the Picts	43
The Goodman of Wastness	45
The Battle of the Birds	48
The Knight of Riddles	59
The Good Housewife	63
The King of Lochlin's Three Daughters	66
The Wife and her Bush of Berries	72
Finn and the Young Hero's Children	77
The Stove Worm	83
Childe Rowland to the Dark Tower Came	85
Jock and his Bagpipes	89

CONTENTS

The Tale of the Hoodie   page 92

The Gael and the London Bailie's Daughter   96

Johnnie Croy and the Mermaid   101

Oscar and the Giant   104

The Young King   106

The White Pet   114

Tam Scott and the Fin-man   118

The Legend of Loch Maree   121

Finn and the Grey Dog   124

The Smith and the Fairies   128

Farquhar the Physician   131

Mally Whuppie   134

The Mermaid   139

Cuchulainn and the Two Giants   148

Glossary   151

The Well at the World's End

THERE was once a King and a Queen. The King had a daughter and the Queen had a daughter. The King's daughter was good-natured and everybody liked her. The Queen's daughter was ill-natured and nobody liked her. Now, the Queen was jealous of the King's daughter, and wished her away. So she sent her to the Well at the World's End to fetch a bottle of water, thinking she would never return.

The King's daughter took a bottle, and away she went. Far she went, till she came to a pony tethered to a tree, and the pony said to her:

> "Free me, free me,
>   My bonny maiden,
> For I haven't been free
>   Seven years and a day."

"Yes I will free you," said the King's daughter.

"Jump on my back," said the pony, "and I'll carry you over the moor of sharp thorns."

The pony took her over the moor of sharp thorns and they parted. She went far, and far, and farther than I can tell, till she came to the Well at the World's End.

She found the Well was very deep, and couldn't dip her bottle. As she was looking down, wondering what to do, she saw three scaly men's heads. Looking up at her, they said:

> "Wash me, wash me,
>   My bonny maiden,
> And dry me with
>   Your clean linen apron."

1

"Yes, I'll wash you," said she.

She washed the three scaly heads, and dried them with her clean linen apron. Then they took and dipped her bottle for her. The three scaly men's heads said one to the other:

"Wish, brother, wish! What will you wish?"

"I wish that if she was bonny before, she'll be ten times bonnier now," said the first.

"I wish that every time she speaks there will drop a ruby, a diamond and a pearl out of her mouth," said the second.

"I wish that every time she combs her hair she'll comb a peck of gold and a peck of silver out of it," said the third.

The King's daughter went home, and if she was bonny before, she was ten times bonnier now. Each time she spoke, a ruby, a diamond and a pearl dropped from her mouth. Each time she combed her hair she combed a peck of gold and a peck of silver out of it.

The Queen was so angry she didn't know what to do. She thought she would send her own daughter to the Well at the World's End to see if she would have the same luck. She gave her a bottle and sent her to fill it with water from the Well.

The Queen's daughter went, and went, till she came to the tethered pony, and the pony said:

> *"Free me, free me,*
> *My bonny maiden,*
> *For I haven't been free*
> *Seven years and a day."*

"Oh, you stupid creature, do you think I'll free you?" said she. "I am the Queen's daughter."

"I'll not carry you, then, over the moor of sharp thorns," said the pony.

So the Queen's daughter had to go on her bare feet, and the thorns cut her. She could scarcely walk at all.

She went far, and far, and farther than I can tell, till she came to the Well at the World's End. But the Well was so deep that she couldn't dip her bottle. As she sat there wondering what to do, there looked up at her three scaly men's heads, and they said:

> *"Wash me, wash me,*
> *My bonny maiden,*
> *And dry me with*
> *Your clean linen apron."*

"Oh, you horrid creatures, do you think I am going to wash you?" said she. "I am the Queen's daughter."

She did not wash their heads, and so they did not dip her bottle for her. They said one to the other:

"Wish, brother, wish! What will you wish?"

"I wish that if she was ugly before, she'll be ten times uglier now," said the first.

"I wish that every time she speaks there will drop a frog and a toad out of her mouth," said the second.

"I wish that every time she combs her hair she'll comb a peck of lice and a peck of fleas out of it," said the third.

So the Queen's daughter went home with an empty bottle. The Queen was mad with rage for, if her daughter had been ugly before, she was ten times uglier now, and when she spoke, a frog and a toad dropped from her mouth. When she combed her hair, a peck of lice and a peck of fleas were combed out of it. So they had to send her away from the Court.

A young Prince came and married the King's daughter, but the Queen's daughter had to put up with an ill-natured cobbler, who beat her every day.

The Wee Bannock

[AYRSHIRE]

THERE lived an old man and an old wife at the side of a burn. They had two cows, five hens and a cock, a cat and two kittens. The old man looked after the cows, and the old wife span on the distaff. The kittens often clawed at the old wife's spindle as it danced over the hearthstone.

"Sho, sho," she said; "go away!" And so it danced about.

One day, after porridge time, she thought she would have a bannock. So she baked two oatmeal bannocks, and set them to the fire to toast. After a while, the old man came in, sat down beside the fire, took up one of the bannocks and snapped it through the middle. When the other one saw this, it ran off as fast as it could, and the old wife after it, with the spindle in one hand and the distaff in the other.

But the wee bannock went away, out of sight, and ran till it came to a fine large thatched house, and in it ran till it came to the fireside. There were three tailors sitting on a big table. When they saw the wee bannock come in, they jumped up and went behind the goodwife, who was carding flax beside the fire.

"Don't be frightened," said she. "It's only a wee bannock. Catch it, and I'll give you a mouthful of milk with it."

Up she got with the flax-cards, and the tailor with the smoothing-iron, and the two apprentices, the one with the big shears and the other with the lap-board. But it dodged them and ran about the fire. One of the apprentices, thinking to snap it with the shears, fell into the ash-pit. The tailor threw the smoothing-iron, and the goodwife the flax-cards, but it was no use. The bannock escaped, and ran till it came to a wee house at the roadside. In it ran, and there was a weaver sitting on the loom, and the wife winding a hank of yarn.

"Tibby," said he, "what's that?"

"Oh," said she, "it's a wee bannock."

"It's welcome," said he, "for our gruel was but thin to-day. Catch it, my woman, catch it!"

"Ay," said she, "if I can. That's a clever bannock. Catch it, Willie! Catch, man!"

"Cast the clew at it!" said Willie.

But the bannock ran round about, across the floor and off over the hill, like a new-tarred sheep or a mad cow. On it ran to the next house, and in it ran to the fireside, where the goodwife was churning.

"Come away, wee bannock," said she. "I'm having cream and bread to-day."

But the wee bannock ran round about the churn, the wife after it, and in the hurry she nearly overturned the churn. Before she had it set right again, the wee bannock was off, down the hillside to the mill, and in it ran.

The miller was sifting meal in the trough, but, looking up, he smiled at the wee bannock.

"Ay," said he, "it's a sign of plenty when you are running about, and nobody to look after you. I like a bannock and cheese. Come away in, and I'll give you a night's quarters."

But the wee bannock would not trust itself with the miller and his cheese. So it ran out of the mill, but the miller didn't trouble his head about it.

It ran and it ran till it came to the smiddy. In it went, and up to the anvil. The smith was making horse-nails.

"I like a cog of good ale, and a well-toasted bannock," said he. "Come away in here."

The bannock was frightened when it heard about the ale, and ran off as hard as it could. The smith ran after it, and threw his hammer. But the bannock whirled away, and was out of sight in an instant. It ran till it came to a farmhouse with a large peat-stack at the end of it. In it ran to the fireside. The goodman was separating lint, and the goodwife was dressing flax.

"Janet," said he, "there's a wee bannock. I'll have the half of it."

"Well, John, I'll have the other half. Hit it over the back with a clew."

The bannock played tig. The old wife threw the heckle at it, but it was too clever for her.

Off and up the stream it ran to the next house, and whirled away in to the fireside. The goodwife was stirring the gruel and the goodman plaiting rush-ropes for the cattle.

"Hey, Jock," said the goodwife, "come here! You are always crying about a bannock. Here's one. Come in, hurry now! I'll help you catch it."

"Ay, wife, where is it?"

"See, there. Run over to that side."

But the wee bannock ran in behind the goodman's chair. Jock fell among the rushes. The goodwife threw the porridge stick and the goodman a rope, but it was too clever for either of them. It was off and out of sight in an instant, through the whins, and down the road to the next house. In it went to the fireside just as the folk were sitting down to their gruel, and the goodwife was scraping the pot.

"Losh," said she, "there's a wee bannock come in to warm itself at our fireside!"

"Fasten the door," said the goodman, "and we'll try to get a grip of it."

When the bannock heard this, it ran into the kitchen, and they after it with their spoons. The goodman threw his bonnet, but it ran, and ran, and faster ran, till it came to another house. When it went in, the folk were just going to their beds. The goodman was casting off his trousers, and the goodwife raking the fire.

"What's that?" said he.

"Oh," said she, "it's a wee bannock."

"I could eat the half of it, for all the porridge I supped," said he.

"Catch it!" said the wife, "and I'll have a bit too. Throw your trousers at it! Kep! Kep!"

The goodman threw his trousers at it, and nearly smothered it. But it wrestled out, and ran, the goodman after it without his trousers. There was a rare chase over the croft field, up the yard and in among the whins. There the goodman lost it, and had to go trotting home half naked. But it had grown dark. The wee bannock couldn't see, went through a whin bush, and right into a fox's hole. The fox had had no meat for two days.

"Welcome, welcome," said the fox, and snapped it in two. And that was the end of the wee bannock.

Rashie Coat

RASHIE COAT was a King's daughter, and her father wanted her to marry, but she did not like the man he had chosen. Her father said she must marry him, so she went to a hen-wife to ask her advice.

"Say you won't take him," said the hen-wife, "unless you are given a coat of beaten gold."

They gave her a coat of beaten gold, but she didn't want him for all that. So she went to the hen-wife again.

"Say you won't take him," said the hen-wife, "unless you are given a coat made of feathers from all the birds of the air."

The King sent a man with a great basket of oats, who called to the birds of the air:

"Each bird take up a grain and put down a feather! Each bird take up a grain and put down a feather!"

So each bird took up a grain and put down a feather, and all the feathers were made into a coat and given to Rashie Coat. But she didn't want him for all that.

She went to the hen-wife and asked her what she should do.

"Say you won't take him unless you are given a coat and slippers made of rushes," said the hen-wife.

The King gave her a coat and slippers made of rushes, but she didn't like him for all that. So she went to the hen-wife again.

"I can't help you any more," said the hen-wife.

Rashie Coat left her father's house and went far, and far, and farther than I can tell, till she came to a King's house.

"What do you want?" said the servants, when she went to the door.

"I would like to work in this house," said she.

So they put her in the kitchen to wash the dishes, and take out the ashes.

When the Sabbath Day came, they all went to the Kirk and left her at home to cook the dinner. While she was alone a fairy came to her, and told her to put on the coat of beaten gold, and go to the Kirk.

"I can't do that," said she, "for I have to cook the dinner."

The fairy told her to go and she would cook the dinner. So Rashie Coat said:

> *"One peat make another peat burn,*
> *One spit make another spit turn,*
> *One pot make another pot play,*
> *Let Rashie Coat go to the Kirk to-day."*

Then she put on her coat of beaten gold, and went to the Kirk. There the King's son saw her and fell in love with her, but she left before everyone else, and he couldn't find out who she was. When she reached home, she found the dinner cooked, and nobody knew she had been out.

The next Sabbath Day the fairy came again, and told her to put on the coat of feathers from all the birds of the air, and to go to the Kirk, for she would cook the dinner for her. So Rashie Coat said:

> *"One peat make another peat burn,*
> *One spit make another spit turn,*
> *One pot make another pot play,*
> *Let Rashie Coat go to the Kirk to-day."*

Then she put on her coat of feathers, and went to the Kirk. Again she left before the others, and when the King's son saw her go out, he followed her. But already she had vanished, and he could not find out who she was. When she reached home, she took off the coat of feathers, and found the dinner cooked. Nobody knew she had been out.

The next Sabbath Day the fairy came once more, and told her to put on the coat of rushes and the pair of slippers, and go to the Kirk while the dinner was being cooked. So Rashie Coat said:

> *"One peat make another peat burn,*
> *One spit make another spit turn,*
> *One pot make another pot play,*
> *Let Rashie Coat go to the Kirk to-day."*

Then she put on her coat of rushes and the pair of slippers, and went to the Kirk.

This time the King's son sat near the door. When he saw Rashie Coat slipping out before everyone else, he followed her at once, but again she was too quick for him, and was nowhere to be seen.

She ran home, but in her haste she lost one of her slippers.

The Prince found the slipper, and sent a Royal Proclamation through all the country, announcing that he would marry whosoever could put on the slipper.

All the ladies of the Court, and their ladies-in-waiting, tried to put on the slipper, and it wouldn't fit any of them, nor the daughters of merchants, farmers and tradesmen who came from far and wide to try their luck. Then the old hen-wife brought her ugly daughter to try it on. She nipped her foot and clipped her foot, and squeezed it on that way. So the King's son said he would marry her.

He was taking her away, riding on a horse, and she behind him, when they came to a wood, and there was a bird sitting on a tree. As they rode by, the bird sang:

> *"Nipped foot and clipped foot*
> *Behind the King's son rides;*
> *But bonny foot and pretty foot*
> *Behind the cauldron hides."*

When the King's son heard this, he flung the hen-wife's daughter off, and went home again. He looked behind the cauldron in the royal kitchen and there he found Rashie Coat. He tried the slipper on her foot and it went on easily. So he married her and they lived happily ever after.

The Flea and the Louse
[SHETLAND]

The Flea and the Louse lived together in a house:
*   And as they shook their sheets,*
The Flea she stumbled and fell in the fire,
*   And now the Louse she weeps.*

The Pot-hook he saw the Louse weeping.

"Louse! Louse! Why are you weeping?"

"Oh! The Flea and I were shaking our sheets:
The Flea she fell and she fell in the fire,
So what can I do but weep?"

"Oh! Then," said the Hook,
"I'll wig-wag back and forward!"

So the Hook wig-wagged, and the Louse she wept.

The Chair saw the Hook wig-wagging.

"Hook! Hook! Why are you wig-wagging?"

"Oh! The Flea and the Louse were shaking their sheets:
The Flea she fell in the fire and burned,
So the Louse she weeps, and I wig-wag."

"Oh! Then," said the Chair,
"I'll jump over the floor."

So the Chair he jumped; the Hook wig-wagged; and the Louse she wept.

The Door he saw the Chair jumping.

"Chair! Chair! Why are you jumping on the floor?"

"Oh! The Flea and the Louse were shaking their sheets:
The Flea she fell in the fire, and the Louse she weeps:
The Hook wig-wags, and so I jump."

"Oh! Then, I'll jingle upon my hinges."

So the Door jingle-jangled; the Chair he jumped; the Hook wig-wagged; and the Louse she wept.

The Midden he saw the Door jingling.

"Door! Door! Why are you jingle-jangling upon your hinges?"

"Oh! The Flea and the Louse were shaking their sheets:
The Flea she fell in the fire, and the Louse she weeps:
The Hook wig-wags: the Chair he jumps,
And I jingle-jangle upon my hinges."

"Oh! Then," said the Midden,
"I'll swarm over with maggots."

So the Midden he swarmed; the Door jingle-jangled; the Chair he jumped; the Hook wig-wagged; and the Louse she wept.

The Burn he saw the Midden swarming.

"Midden! Midden! Why are you swarming over with maggots?"

"Oh! The Flea and the Louse were shaking their sheets:
The Flea she fell in the fire, and the Louse she weeps:
The Hook wig-wags: the Chair he jumps:
The Door jingle-jangles, and I swarm over with maggots."

"Oh! Then, I'll run wimple-wample."

So the Burn ran wimple-wample; the Midden he

swarmed; the Door he jingled; the Chair he jumped; the Hook wig-wagged; and the Louse she wept.

The Loch saw the Burn running wimple-wample.

"Burn! Burn! Why are you running wimple-wample?"

"Oh! The Flea and the Louse were shaking their sheets:
The Flea she fell in the fire, and the Louse she weeps:
The Hook wig-wags: the Chair he jumps:
The Door jingle-jangles: the Midden swarms over with
*   maggots,*
And I run wimple-wample."

"Oh! Then, I'll swell over my brim."

So the Loch he swelled and he swelled; the Burn ran wimple-wample; the Midden he swarmed; the Door he jingled; the Chair he jumped; the Hook wig-wagged; and the Louse she wept.

Then down came the flood and swept away the House and the Louse, the Hook and the Chair, the Door and the Midden, with the Maggots—all down into the meadow where the Burn ran wimple-wample.

So ends the story of the Flea and the Louse.

Whuppity Stoorie

[DUMFRIESSHIRE]

THE goodman of Kittlerumpit was a bit of a vagabond.
He went to the fair one day and was never heard of
again.

When the goodman had gone, the goodwife was left with
little to live on. Few belongings she had, and a wee son.
Everybody said they were sorry for her, but nobody
helped her. However, she had a sow, that was her consola-
tion, for the sow was soon to farrow, and she hoped for a
fine litter of piglets.

But one day, when the wife went to the sty to fill the
sow's trough, what did she find but the sow lying on her
back, grunting and groaning, and ready to die.

This was a blow to the goodwife, so she sat down on the
knocking stone, with her bairn on her knee, and wept more
sorely than she did for the loss of her goodman.

Now, the cottage of Kittlerumpit was built on a brae, with a fir-wood behind it. So, as the goodwife was wiping her eyes, what did she see but an old woman coming up the brae. She was dressed in green, all but a white apron, a black velvet hood, and a steeple-crowned hat on her head. She had a walking-stick as long as herself in her hand.

When the Green Lady drew near, the goodwife rose and made a curtsy.

"Madam," said she, "I'm the most unlucky woman alive."

"I don't want to hear piper's news and fiddler's tales," said the Green Lady. "I know you've lost your goodman, and your sow is sick. Now, what will you give me if I cure her?"

"Anything you like," said the stupid goodwife, not guessing who she had to deal with.

"Let's wet thumbs on that bargain," said the Green Lady.

So thumbs were wet, and into the sty she marched.

The Green Lady looked at the sow with a frown, and then began to mutter to herself words the goodwife couldn't understand, but sounded like,

> "*Pitter patter,*
> *Haly watter.*"

Then she took out of her pocket a wee bottle with something like oil in it, and rubbed the sow with it above the snout, behind the ears and on the top of the tail.

"Get up, beast," said the Green Lady. Up got the sow with a grunt, and away to her trough for her breakfast.

The goodwife of Kittlerumpit was overjoyed when she saw that.

"Now that I've cured your sick beast, let us carry out our bargain," said the Green Lady. "You'll not find me unreasonable. I always like to do a good turn for small reward. All I ask, and WILL have, is that wee son in your arms."

The goodwife gave a shriek like a stuck pig, for she now knew that the Green Lady was a fairy. So she wept, and she begged, but it was no use.

"You can spare your row," said the fairy, "shrieking as if I was as deaf as a door nail; but I can't, by the law we live by, take your bairn till the third day after this; and not then, if you can tell me my name."

With that the fairy went away down the brae and out of sight.

The goodwife of Kittlerumpit could not sleep that night for weeping, holding her bairn so tight that she nearly squeezed the breath out of him.

The next day she went for a walk in the wood behind her cottage. Her bairn in her arms, she went far among the trees till she came to an old quarry overgrown with grass, and a bonny spring well in the middle of it. As she drew near, she heard the whirring of a spinning-wheel, and a voice singing a song. So the wife crept quietly among the bushes, peeped over the side of the quarry, and what did she see but the Green Lady at her spinning-wheel singing:

> "*Little kens our goodwife at hame*
> *That* WHUPPITY STOORIE *is my name!*"

"Ah, ah!" thought the goodwife, "I've got the secret word at last!"

So she went home with a lighter heart than when she came out, laughing at the thought of tricking the fairy.

This goodwife was a merry woman, so she decided to have some sport with the fairy. At the appointed time she put the bairn behind the knocking stone, and sat down on it herself. She pulled her cap awry over her left ear, twisted her mouth on the other side as if she were weeping. She hadn't long to wait, for up the brae came the fairy, neither lame nor lazy, and long before she reached the knocking stone she skirled out:

"Goodwife of Kittlerumpit! You well know what I have come for!"

The goodwife pretended to weep more bitterly than before, wringing her hands and falling on her knees.

"Och, dear mistress," said she, "spare my only bairn and take the weary sow!"

"The deil take the sow for my share," said the fairy. "I didn't come here for swine's flesh. Don't be contrary, goodwife, but give me the child instantly!"

"Ochon, dear lady," said the weeping goodwife, "give up my bairn and take myself!"

"The deil's in the daft woman," said the fairy, looking like the far end of a fiddle. "I'm sure she's clean demented. Who in all the earthly world, with half an eye in their head, would be bothered with the likes of you?"

This made the goodwife of Kittlerumpit bristle; for though she had two bleary eyes, and a long red nose besides, she thought herself as bonny as the best of them. She soon got up off her knees, set her cap straight, and with her hands folded before her, she made a curtsy down to the ground.

"I might have known," said she, "that the likes of me isn't fit to tie the shoe-strings of the high and mighty fairy WHUPPITY STOORIE!"

The name made the fairy leap high. Down she came again, dump on her heels, and whirling round, she ran down the hill like an owlet chased by witches.

The goodwife of Kittlerumpit laughed till she nearly burst. Then she took up her bairn and went into her house, singing to him all the way:

> "Coo and gurgle, my bonny wee tyke,
>   You'll now have your four-houries
> Since we've gien Nick a bone to pick,
>   With his wheels and his WHUPPITY STOORIES."

The Winning of Hyn-Hallow
[ORKNEY]

THERE was once a goodman of Thorodale. He married a wife, who had three sons by him, and then she died. After a year had passed, he married a young lass in the parish of Evie, and loved her with all his heart.

One day they were down in the ebb, when Thorodale stopped to tie his boot-lace. His back was to his young wife, when suddenly she screamed. A tall, dark man dragged her into a boat, and pushed out to sea before Thorodale could reach them. Thorodale never saw his wife again.

He pulled up his breeches, took down his stockings, and went on his knees below flood-mark. There he swore that, living or dead, he would be revenged on the Fin-folk.

One day he was out fishing on the sound that lies between Rousay and Evie, when he heard a woman's voice singing. He knew it was his wife, although he could not see her, for she sang:

> "Goodman, weep no more for me,
> For me again you'll never see.
> If you would have of vengeance joy,
> Go speir the wise speywife of Hoy."

Thorodale went ashore, took his staff in his hand, his silver in a stocking, and set off for the island of Hoy. There the old speywife told him how he might get the power of seeing Hilda-land, and how he was to act when he saw it.

Thorodale returned home and for nine months at midnight, when the moon was full, he went nine times on his bare knees round the Odin Stone of Stainess. For nine months, at full moon, he looked through the hole in the Odin Stone, and wished that he might have the power of seeing

Hilda-land. He filled a girnal with salt, and set three baskets beside it; he then told his three grown-up sons what they must do when he gave them the word.

One summer morning, just after sunrise, Thorodale saw a little island in the middle of the sound where he had never seen land before. He could not turn his head, nor wink his eye, for if he once lost sight of that land he knew he would not see it again. So he shouted to his three sons in the house:

"Fill the baskets with salt, and hold for the boat!"

The sons came, each carrying a basket of salt. The four men jumped in, and rowed the boat for the new land, although nobody saw it except the goodman.

In a moment, the boat was surrounded by whales. The three sons wanted to drive the whales away, but their father cried:

"Pull for dear life!"

A great whale lay right in the boat's course, and opened up a mouth big enough to swallow boat and men. Thorodale, standing in the bow of his boat, flung two handfuls of salt into its mouth, and the whale vanished.

As the boat neared the shore of Hilda-land, two mermaids stood on the rocks and sang. The young men began to row slowly. Thorodale gave his sons a kick, without turning his head, and cried to the mermaids:

"Begone, you unholy creatures! Here's your warning!"

He threw a cross of twisted seaweed on them, and the mermaids sprang screaming into the sea.

When the boat touched land, they saw a great monster with long tusks, and feet as broad as millstones. Its eyes blazed and its mouth spat fire. Thorodale flung a handful of salt between the monster's eyes, and it disappeared with a roar. A tall man with a drawn sword stood there.

"Go back, you human thieves! or I'll defile Hilda-land with your blood!"

The three sons began to tremble.

"Come home, Father, come home!" they cried.

The tall man thrust at Thorodale with his sword, but Thorodale flung a cross of cloggirs on his face. The tall man turned and fled in pain and anger.

"Come out of that," cried Thorodale to his sons, "and take the salt ashore!"

Their father made them walk abreast round the island, each man scattering salt as he went.

There arose a terrible rumpus among the Fin-folk and their kye. They ran helter-skelter into the sea, like a flock of sheep, and never set foot on Hyn-hallow again.

Thorodale cut nine crosses on the turf, and his sons went three times round the island sowing their salt. But the youngest son had a large hand, and sowed the salt too fast. Not a particle would his brothers spare him, so the ninth circle of salt was never completed. That is why cats, rats and mice cannot live on Hyn-hallow.

In the Orkneys they still sing:

> *"Hyn-hallow frank, Hyn-hallow free!*
> *Hyn-hallow lies in the middle of the sea;*
> *Wi a rampan rost on ilka side,*
> *Hyn-hallow lies in the middle of the tide."*

The Maiden Fair and the Fountain Fairy

[DUMFRIESSHIRE]

LONG, long ago a drover courted and married the miller of Cuthilldorie's only daughter. By the time the miller died, the drover had learned the trade and with his young wife set up as the miller of Cuthilldorie. He hadn't much silver to begin with, but an old Highland drover he knew lent him some.

By and by the young miller and his wife had a daughter, but on the very night she was born the fairies stole her away. The wee thing was carried far away from the house into the wood of Cuthilldorie, where she was found on the very lip of the Black Well. In the air was heard a lilting:

"O we'll come back again, my honey, my hert,
We'll come back again, my ain kind dearie;
And you will mind upon the time
When we met in the wood at the Well so wearie!"

The lassie grew up to be by far the bonniest lass in all the countryside. Everything went well at the mill.

One dark night there came a wood-cock with a glowing tinder in its beak, and set fire to the mill. Everything was burnt and the miller was left without a thing in the world. To make matters worse, who should come next morning but the old drover who had lent them the silver, saying he had not been paid.

Now, there was a wee old man in the wood of Cuthilldorie beside the Black Well who would never stay in a house if he could help it. In the winter he went away, nobody knew where. He was an ugly bogle, not above two and a half feet high.

He had been seen only three times in the fifteen years since he came to the place, for he always flew up out of sight when anybody came near him. But if you had crept cannily through the wood after dark, you might have heard him playing with the water, and singing the same song:

> "*O when will you come, my honey, my hert,*
> *O when will you come, my ain kind dearie;*
> *For don't you mind upon the time*
> *We met in the wood at the Well so wearie?*"

Well, the night after the firing of the mill, the miller's daughter wandered into the wood alone, and wandered and wandered till she came to the Black Well. Then the wee bogle gripped her and jumped about singing:

> "*O come with me, my honey, my hert,*
> *O come you with me, my ain kind dearie;*
> *For don't you mind upon the time*
> *We met in the wood at the Well so wearie?*"

With that he made her drink three double handfuls of the witched water, and away they flew on a flash of lightning. When the poor lass opened her eyes, she was in the middle of a palace, all gold and silver and diamonds, and full of fairies.

The King and Queen invited her to stay, and said she would be well looked after. But if she wanted to go home again, she must never tell anybody where she had been or what she had seen.

She said she wanted to go home, and promised to do as she was bidden.

Then the King said:

"The first stranger you meet, give him brose!"

"Give him bannocks!" said the Queen.

"Give him butter!" said the King.

"Give him a drink of the Black Well water!" they both said together.

Then they gave her twelve drops of liquid in a wee green bottle, three drops for the brose, three for the bannocks, three for the butter and three for the Black Well water.

She took the green bottle in her hand, and suddenly it was

dark. She was flying through the air, and when she opened her eyes she was at her own doorstep. She slipped away to her bed, glad to be home again, and said nothing about where she had been or what she had seen.

Next morning, before the sun was up, there came a rap,

rap, rap, three times at the door. The sleepy lass looked out and saw an old beggar-man, who began to sing:

> "*O open the door, my honey, my hert,*
>   *O open the door, my ain kind dearie;*
> *For don't you mind upon the time*
>   *We met in the wood at the Well so wearie?*"

When she heard that, she said nothing, and opened the door. The old beggar came in, singing:

> "*O gie me my brose, my honey, my hert,*
>   *O gie me my brose, my ain kind dearie;*
> *For don't you mind upon the time*
>   *We met in the wood at the Well so wearie?*"

The lassie made a bicker of brose for the beggar, not forgetting the three drops of the green bottle. As he was supping the brose he vanished, and there was the big Highland drover, who lent the silver to the miller, singing:

> "*O gie me my bannocks, my honey, my hert,*
>   *O gie me my bannocks, my ain kind dearie;*
> *For don't you mind upon the time*
>   *We met in the wood at the Well so wearie?*"

She baked him some fresh bannocks, not forgetting the three drops from the wee green bottle. He had just finished eating the bannocks when he vanished, and there was the wood-cock that fired the mill, singing:

> "*O gie me my butter, my honey, my hert,*
>   *O gie me my butter, my ain kind dearie;*
> *For don't you mind upon the time*
>   *We met in the wood at the Well so wearie?*"

She gave him butter as fast as she could, not forgetting the three drops from the green bottle. He had only eaten a bite, when he flapped his wings and vanished, and there was the ugly wee bogle that gripped her at the Black Well the night before, singing:

"O gie me my water, my honey, my hert,
   O gie me my water, my ain kind dearie;
For don't you mind upon the time
   We met in the wood at the Well so wearie?"

She knew there were only three other drops in the green bottle and she was afraid. She ran as fast as she could to the Black Well, but who should be there before her but the wee ugly bogle himself, singing:

"O gie me my water, my honey, my hert,
   O gie me my water, my ain kind dearie;
For don't you mind upon the time
   We met in the wood at the Well so wearie?"

She gave him the water, not forgetting the three drops from the green bottle. But he had scarcely drunk the witched water when he vanished, and there was a fine young Prince, who spoke to her as if he had known her all her days.

They sat down beside the Black Well.

"I was born the same night as you," he said, "and I was carried away by the fairies the same night as you were found on the lip of the Well. I was a bogle for so many years because the fairies were scared away. They made me play many tricks before they would let me go, and return to my father, the King of France, and make the bonniest lass in all the world my bride."

"Who is she?" said the maiden.

"The miller of Cuthilldorie's daughter," said the young Prince.

Then they went home and told their stories over again, and that very night they were married. A coach-and-four came for them, and the miller and his wife, and the Prince and the Princess, drove away singing:

"*O but we're happy, my honey, my hert,*
    O but we're happy, my ain kind dearie;
  For don't you mind upon the time
    When we met in the wood at the Well so wearie?"

The Tale of the Soldier

[WEST HIGHLANDS]

ONCE there was an old soldier who had deserted from the army. He climbed a hill at the top end of the town.

"May the Mischief carry me away on his back the next time I come within sight of this town," he said.

He walked till he came to a gentleman's house.

"May I stay in your house to-night?" he asked.

"You are an old soldier with the look of a brave man," said the gentleman. "You may stay in the castle beside that wood till morning. You will have a pipe and tobacco, a cogie of whisky, and a Bible."

After supper, John went to the castle and lit a big fire. When part of the night had gone, two brown women came in carrying a chest. They put it by the fireside and went out. With the heel of his boot John stove in the end of it, and pulled out an old grey man. He sat the man in the big chair, gave him a pipe and tobacco, and a cogie of whisky, but the old man let them fall on the floor.

"Poor man," said John, "you're cold."

John stretched himself on the bed, and left the old man to warm himself at the fire, where he stayed till the cock crew, then took himself off.

The gentleman came in the morning early.

"Did you sleep well?" he asked.

"Very well," said John. "Your father wasn't the kind of man to frighten me."

"I'll give you two hundred pounds if you stay in the castle to-night."

"I'll do that," said John.

The same thing happened that night. Three brown

29

women came in carrying a chest. They put it by the fireside and went out. With the heel of his boot John stove in the end of it, and pulled out the old grey man. As he did the night before, he sat the man in the big chair and gave him a pipe and tobacco. He let them fall.

"Poor man," said John, "you're cold."

He gave him a cogie of drink, and he let that fall. Then the old man went away, as he did the night before.

"If I stay here to-night, and you come," said John to himself, "you'll pay for my pipe and tobacco, and my cogie of drink."

The gentleman came in the morning early.

"Did you sleep well last night, John?"

"Very well," said John. "Your old father wasn't the kind of man to frighten me."

"If you stay to-night, you shall have three hundred pounds."

"That's a bargain," said John.

When part of the night had gone, four brown women came, carrying a chest, and put it down beside John. He stove in the end of the chest with his boot, pulled out the old grey man, and sat him in the big chair. He gave him the pipe and tobacco, the cogie and the drink, but the old man dropped them and broke the pipe and cup.

"Before you go to-night, you'll pay me for all you've broken," said John.

The old man said nothing. John took the strap of his haversack, tied the old man to his side, and took him to bed with him. When the cock crew, the old man begged him to let him go.

"Pay for what you've broken first," said John.

"I'll tell you then," said the old man. "There's a wine-cellar down there, and in it there's plenty drink, tobacco and pipes. There's another little room beside the cellar, and in it there's a pot full of gold. Under the threshold of the big door there's a crock full of silver. Did you see the women that brought me to-night?"

"I did," said John.

"They are the four very poor women from whom I stole the cows. These women carry me every night this way, to punish me. Go and tell my son how I am being tired out. Let him go and pay for the cows, and not be hard on the poor. You and he divide the gold between you, and you marry my old widow. But remember, give plenty of what is left to the poor. I was too hard on them. And I'll find rest in the next world."

The gentleman came, and John told him what I have told you. But John would not marry the widow of the old grey man.

After a day or two, John would not stay any longer. He filled his pockets with gold, and asked the gentleman to give plenty of gold to the poor.

He went home, but he wearied there, and would rather have been back with the regiment. One day he went away till he reached the hill at the top of the town. And who should meet him but the Mischief!

"You've come back, John?"

"I've come back, but who are you?"

"I'm the Mischief. You gave yourself to me when you were here last."

"I've heard tell of you," said John, "but I never saw you before. My eyes are deceiving me. I don't believe it's you at all, but make yourself into a snake and I'll believe you."

The Mischief did so.

"Now, make yourself into a roaring lion."

The Mischief did so.

"Spit fire now, seven miles in front of you and seven miles behind you."

The Mischief did so.

"Well," said John, "if I'm to be your servant, go into my

haversack and I'll carry you. But you mustn't come out till I tell you, or the bargain's broken."

The Mischief promised, and did what he was told.

"I'm going to see my brother in the regiment," said John, "but keep quiet."

John went into the town, and one man here and another man there cried, "There's John, the deserter!"

They arrested John, and tried him in court. He was sentenced to be hanged next day, at noon. John said he preferred to be shot.

"Since you're an old soldier, and have been a long time in the army, you shall have your wish," said the Colonel.

Next day, John was about to be shot, and the soldiers were all round him.

"What's that they're saying?" said the Mischief. "Let me get among them, and I'll not be long in scattering them."

"Hush, hush," said John.

"Who's that speaking to you?" said the Colonel.

"Oh, it's only a white mouse," said John.

"Black or white," said the Colonel, "don't let it out of the haversack, and you shall have your discharge from the army. Let us see no more of you."

John went away, and at dusk he went into a barn where twelve men were threshing.

"Here's my old haversack for you, lads," said John. "Thresh it for a while. It's so hard, it's taking the skin off my back."

For two hours they threshed the haversack with the twelve flails. At last every blow they gave it made it jump to the roof of the barn. Now and then it threw a thresher on his back. When they saw that, they told him to be out of that, him and his haversack. They wouldn't believe but the Mischief was in it.

Then he went on his way, and entered a smiddy, where twelve blacksmiths were using their big hammers.

"Here's an old haversack for you, lads. I'll give you half a crown. Hammer it for a while with your twelve big hammers. It's so hard, it's taking the skin off my back."

The soldier's haversack was good sport for the blacksmiths, but every blow it got it jumped to the roof of the smiddy.

"Get out of this, yourself and it," they said. "We believe the Brahman's in it."

John went on, and the Mischief on his back. He reached a great furnace.

"Where are you going now, John?" said the Mischief.

"A little patience, and you'll see," said John.

"Let me out," said the Mischief, "and I'll never trouble you again in this world."

"Nor in the next?" said John.

"I agree," said the Mischief.

John threw the haversack, and the Mischief, into the middle of the furnace, and he and the furnace went up in a green flame to the sky.

Pippety Pew

[LOWLANDS]

THERE once was a man who worked in the fields, and he had a wife, a son and a daughter. One day he caught a hare, took it home to his wife and bade her make it ready for his dinner.

While it was on the fire cooking, the goodwife kept on tasting it, till she had tasted it all away, and she didn't know what to do for her husband's dinner. So she called Johnnie, her son, to come and have his head combed. When she was combing his head she slew him, and put him into the pot.

The goodman came home to his dinner, and his wife set down Johnnie to him, well boiled. When he was eating, he took up a foot.

"Surely that's my Johnnie's foot," said he.

"Nonsense! It's one of the hare's," said she.

Then he took up a hand.

"That's surely my Johnnie's hand," said he.

34

"You're talking nonsense, goodman," said she. "That's another of the hare's feet."

When the goodman had eaten his dinner, his daughter Katy gathered all the bones and put them below the stone at the cheek of the door,

> *Where they grew, and they grew,*
> *To a milk-white doo,*
> *That took its wings,*
> *And away it flew.*

It flew till it came to a burn where two women were washing clothes. It sat down on a stone, and cried:

> *"Pippety Pew!*
> *My mammy me slew,*
> *My daddy me ate,*
> *My sister Kate*
> *Gathered all my banes,*
> *And laid them between*
> *Two milk-white stanes.*
> *So a bird I grew,*
> *And away I flew,*
> *Sing Pippety Pew!"*

"Say that again, my pretty bird, and we'll give you all these clothes," said one of the women.

> *"Pippety Pew!*
> *My mammy me slew,*
> *My daddy me ate,*
> *My sister Kate*
> *Gathered all my banes,*
> *And laid them between*
> *Two milk-white stanes.*

35

> *So a bird I grew,*
> *And away I flew,*
> *Sing Pippety Pew!"*

It took the clothes, and away it flew till it came to a man counting a great heap of silver. It sat down beside him and cried:

> *"Pippety Pew!*
> *My mammy me slew,*
> *My daddy me ate,*
> *My sister Kate*
> *Gathered all my banes,*
> *And laid them between*
> *Two milk-white stanes.*
> *So a bird I grew,*
> *And away I flew,*
> *Sing Pippety Pew!"*

"Say that again, my bonny bird, and I'll give you all this silver," said the man.

> *"Pippety Pew!*
> *My mammy me slew,*
> *My daddy me ate,*
> *My sister Kate*
> *Gathered all my banes,*
> *And laid them between*
> *Two milk-white stanes.*
> *So a bird I grew,*
> *And away I flew,*
> *Sing Pippety Pew!"*

The man gave it all the silver. It flew till it came to a miller grinding corn, and cried:

> *"Pippety Pew!*
> *My mammy me slew,*
> *My daddy me ate,*
> *My sister Kate*
> *Gathered all my banes,*
> *And laid them between*
> *Two milk-white stanes.*
> *So a bird I grew,*
> *And away I flew,*
> *Sing Pippety Pew!"*

"Say that again, my bonny bird, and I'll give you this millstone," said the miller.

> *"Pippety Pew!*
> *My mammy me slew,*
> *My daddy me ate,*
> *My sister Kate*
> *Gathered all my banes,*
> *And laid them between*
> *Two milk-white stanes.*
> *So a bird I grew,*
> *And away I flew,*
> *Sing Pippety Pew!"*

The miller gave it the millstone, and away it flew till it lighted on its father's housetop. It threw small stones down the chimney, and Katy came out to see what was the matter. The dove threw down all the clothes to her. Then the father came out, and the dove threw all the silver down to him. Then the mother came out. The dove threw the millstone down on her, and killed her.

Then the dove flew away, and after that the goodman and his daughter lived happy, and died happy.

The Black Bull of Norroway

I N Norroway, long ago, there lived a lady, and she had three daughters. The eldest of them said to her mother: "Mother, bake me an oatcake, and roast me a collop, for I am going away to seek my fortune."

Her mother did so, and her daughter went to an old speywife to tell her what she was going to do. The speywife bade her look out of the back door and see what she could see.

She saw nothing the first day, and she saw nothing the second day. But on the third day she looked out again and saw a coach-and-six coming along the road. She ran in and told the speywife.

"Well," said the old wife, "that's for you."

So she stepped into the coach, and off she went.

The second daughter then said to her mother:

"Mother, bake me an oatcake, and roast me a collop, for I am going away to seek my fortune."

Her mother did so, and away she went to the old speywife, as her sister had done. On the third day she looked out and saw a coach-and-four coming along the road.

"That's for you," said the old wife.

They took her into the coach, and off they went.

Then the third daughter went to her mother, and said:

"Mother, bake me an oatcake, and roast me a collop, for I am going away to seek my fortune."

Her mother did so, and away she went to the old witchwife, who bade her look out of the back door to see what she could see.

She saw nothing on the first day, and she saw nothing on the second day. But on the third day she looked again, and came back and told the old wife she could see nothing but a great Black Bull coming roaring along the road.

"Well," said the old wife, "that's for you."

When she heard this the poor lass was almost out of her mind with grief and terror. But she was lifted up, set on the Black Bull's back, and away they went.

Long they travelled, and on they travelled, till the lass grew faint with hunger.

"Eat out of my right ear," said the Black Bull, "drink out of my left ear, and set aside your leavings."

She did as he said, and was refreshed.

Long they travelled, and hard they rode, till they came in sight of a castle.

"Yonder we must be this night," said the Bull, "for my brother lives there."

Soon they were at the place. Servants lifted her off his back, took her in, and sent him to a field for the night.

In the morning, when they brought the Bull to the castle, they took the maiden into a fine room, and gave her an apple. They told her not to break it till she was in the greatest strait a mortal could be in, and it would help her.

Again she was lifted on to the Bull's back, and after they had ridden far, and far, and farther than I can tell, they came in sight of another castle, farther away than the last.

"Yonder we must be to-night," said the Black Bull, "for my second brother lives there."

Soon they were at the place. Servants lifted her down, took her in, and sent the Bull to a field for the night.

In the morning they took the maiden into a fine rich room and gave her a pear. They bade her not to open it until she was in the greatest strait a mortal could be in, and it would help her.

Once more she was lifted up and set on the Bull's back, and away they went. Long they rode, and hard they rode, till they came in sight of the grandest castle they had yet seen.

"Yonder we must be to-night," said the Bull, "for my youngest brother lives there."

They were there directly. Servants lifted her down, took her in, and sent the Bull to a field for the night.

In the morning they took her into the finest room of all, and gave her a plum, telling her not to break it until she was in the greatest strait a mortal could be in, and it would help her.

Then the maiden was set on the Bull's back, and away they went.

Long they rode, and on they rode, till they came to a dark and ugly glen. There they stopped, and she alighted.

"Here you must stay," said the Black Bull, "till I go and fight the devil. Seat yourself on that stone, and move neither hand nor foot till I come back, or I'll never find you again. If everything about you turns blue, I'll have beaten the devil; but if everything turns red, he'll have conquered me."

She sat down on a stone, and by and by everything around her turned blue. Overcome with joy, she lifted one foot and crossed it over the other.

The Black Bull returned and looked for the lass, but could not find her.

Long she sat, and wept, until she was wearied. At last she rose and went sadly away, not knowing where she was going. On she wandered, till she came to a great hill of glass that she tried to climb, but could not. Round the bottom of the hill she went seeking a path over it, till at last she came to a smiddy. The blacksmith promised, if she would serve him seven years, to make her a pair of iron shoes, and with these she would be able to climb over the glass mountain.

At the end of seven years she was given the iron shoes. She climbed the glass hill, and came to an old washerwife's cottage. There she was told of a gallant young knight who had given her some blood-stained shirts to be washed. He had said that she who washed his shirts clean would be his bride.

The old wife had washed till she was tired, and then she set her daughter to it. They both washed, and they washed, and they washed, in hopes of winning the young knight; but do what they might, they couldn't take out a single stain.

At length they set the stranger lass to work and, as soon as she began, the stains came out, leaving the shirts clean and white. The old wife told the young knight that her daughter had washed the shirts.

So the knight and the washerwife's daughter were to be married and the stranger lass was distracted at the thought of it, for she was in love with him. Then she remembered her apple, and breaking it, found it full of gold and precious jewellery, the richest she had ever seen.

"All these," she said to the washerwife's daughter, "I will give you, if you put off your marriage for one day, and allow me to go into his room alone to-night."

The daughter agreed but told her mother, who prepared a sleeping draught, and gave it to the knight. He drank it, and slept till next morning. All night long the poor lass wept and sang:

> *"Seven long years I served for you,*
> *The glassy hill I climbed for you,*
> *The blood-stained shirt I wrung for you,*
> *Will ye not waken and turn to me?"*

Next day she did not know what to do. She then remembered the pear, so she broke it, and found it filled with jewellery richer than before. With these she bargained to be a second night in his room. But the old wife gave him another sleeping draught, and he slept till morning.

All night long she sang as before:

> *"Seven long years I served for you,*
> *The glassy hill I climbed for you,*
> *The blood-stained shirt I wrung for you,*
> *Will you not waken and turn to me?"*

Still he slept, and she nearly lost hope. But that day, when he was out hunting, someone asked him what moaning it was they had heard all night in his room. He had not heard a sound himself, but he made up his mind to keep awake that night.

The poor lass, between hope and despair, broke open her plum and it held the richest jewels of the three. She bargained as before, and the old wife took the sleeping draught to the knight. But this time he told her he couldn't drink it without sweetening. When she went to fetch the honey, he poured out the drink, and pretended he had already drunk it.

When everyone was in bed, the lass sang in his room as before:

> *"Seven long years I served for you,*
> *The glassy hill I climbed for you,*
> *The blood-stained shirt I wrung for you,*
> *Will you not waken and turn to me?"*

The knight heard, and turned to her. She told him all that had happened to her and he told her all that had happened to him. After the old wife and her daughter were punished, they were married and lived happily ever after.

The Last of the Picts
[LOWLANDS]

LONG ago there were folks in this country called the Picts. Wee short men they were, with red hair, long arms, and feet so broad that when it rained they could turn them up over their heads for umbrellas.

The Picts were great folk for the ale they brewed from the heather. Many wanted to know how they made it, but the Picts would not give away the secret, handing it down from one to the other.

Then the Picts were at war with the rest of the country, and many of them were killed. Soon only a handful of them were left, and they fought a great battle with the Scots. They lost the battle, and all but two of them were killed. These two were father and son.

The King of the Scots had these men brought before him, to frighten them into telling him the secret of the heather ale. He told them, if they did not reveal the secret, he must torture them.

"Well," said the older man to the King, "I see it is useless to resist. But one condition you must agree to before you learn the secret."

"What is that?" said the King.

"Will you promise to fulfil it if it does not harm you?" said the man.

"I will," said the King, "and promise to do so."

"Then," said the Pict,

> *"My son you must kill*
> *Ere I will you tell*
> *How we brew the yill*
> *From the heather bell!"*

The King was astonished, but he ordered the lad to be put to death immediately.

When the Pict saw that his son was dead, he stood up before the King, and cried:

"Now do what you like with me. You might have forced my son, for he was but a weak youth, but you will never force me.

> *And though you may me kill,*
> *I will not you tell*
> *How we brew the yill*
> *From the heather bell.*"

The King was astonished, and angry that he had been outwitted by a mere wild man. It was useless to kill him, so the Pict was thrown into prison.

The Pict lived until he was an old, old man, bedridden and blind. Most folk had forgotten he was alive, but one night some youths sharing his cell boasted about their feats of strength. The old man leaned out of bed and stretched his hand toward them.

"Let me feel your wrists," he said, "and compare them with the arms of the Picts."

For sport, they held out a thick bar of iron. He snapped it in two with his fingers as though it was a clay-pipe stem.

"It is rather gristly," said he, "but nothing to the wrist-bones of my day."

The Goodman of Wastness

[ORKNEY]

ONE day, when the goodman of Wastness was down
on the ebb, he saw a number of Selkie folk on a flat
rock. They had taken off their seal-skins, and had
skins as white as his own.

The goodman of Wastness crept forward and dashed to
the rock. The Selkie folk seized their skins and jumped into

45

the sea. But the goodman took one of the skins belonging to a Selkie lass.

The Selkie folk swam out a little distance, put their heads out of the water and gazed at the goodman. One of them did not look like a seal.

The goodman put the seal-skin under his arm, and made for home. Before he got out of the ebb, he heard a sound of weeping behind him. The maiden whose seal-skin he had taken was following him.

"If there is any mercy in you, give me back my skin!" she cried. "I cannot bide in the sea, among my own folk, without it. Pity me, if you ever hope for mercy yourself."

"It would be better if you came to bide with me," said the goodman.

After a deal of persuasion, the sea-lass consented to be his wife.

She stayed with him many moons, bore him seven children, four boys and three girls. But although the good-wife of Wastness looked happy, and was often merry, her heart was heavy. Many times she looked long at the sea. She taught her bairns many a strange song that had never been heard before.

One day the goodman of Wastness and his three eldest sons went off in his boat to the fishing. The goodwife sent three of the children to the ebb to gather limpets and whelks, but the youngest, having hurt her foot, had to stay at home. The goodwife began to search for her lost skin.

She searched up, and she searched down. She searched but, and she searched ben. Never a seal-skin could she find. The youngest lass sat on a stool resting her foot.

"What are you looking for, Mam?" she said.

"I am looking for a bonny skin, to make a shoe to cure your sore foot."

"Maybe I know where it is," said the lass. "One day when you were all out, and father thought I was sleeping, he took the bonny skin down. He glowered at it a peerie minute, then folded it and laid it up there between the wall and the roof."

When her mother heard this she rushed to the place and pulled out her long-lost skin.

"Farewell, wee buddo!" she cried, and ran out of the house. She ran to the shore, put on her skin, and plunged into the sea.

There a Selkie man met her and they swam away together. The goodman, rowing home, saw them both from his boat. His lost wife uncovered her face, and cried:

> *"Goodman of Wastness, farewell to ye!*
> *I liked ye well, ye were good to me;*
> *But I love better my man of the sea!"*

That was the last the goodman of Wastness ever saw or heard of his wife.

The Battle of the Birds
[DUMFRIESSHIRE]

ONCE upon a time all the animals and birds were at war. The King's son went to see the battle. He saw one fight between a black raven and a snake, and to help the raven he cut the snake's head off.

"For your kindness to me," said the raven, "I'll let you see something. Come up between my two wings."

The King's son mounted the raven's back, and was carried over seven bens, seven glens and seven mountain moors.

"Now," said the raven, "you see that house there? Go there and tell my sister you saw me at the battle of the birds. But be sure to meet me here to-morrow morning."

"I'll do that," said the King's son.

He was well treated that night, with the best meat and drink, and warm water for his feet, and a soft bed to lie on.

Next day the raven took him over seven bens, seven glens and seven mountain moors. They saw a house belonging to the raven's second sister, and the Prince was well treated, with plenty of meat and drink, warm water for his feet, and a soft bed to lie on.

Next morning he was again met by the raven, and taken over seven bens, seven glens and seven mountain moors. He was well treated by the raven's third sister, but on the third morning, instead of a raven, there was a young man with a bundle in his hand awaiting him.

"Have you seen a raven, young man?" said the Prince.

"I am that raven," said the young man. "You loosed me from a spell, and for that I give you this bundle. Retrace your steps, lie a night at each house as before, but do not open this bundle till you are at the place where you would most like to live."

The Prince retraced his steps. He stayed with the raven's three sisters as before. But as he was going through a deep wood the bundle grew heavy, and he looked to see what was in it.

In an instant, a great castle sprang up, with an orchard filled with every kind of fruit and herb, and every kind of flower grew in its gardens. The castle was in the wrong place, but the King's son could not put it back in the bundle.

Looking round, he saw a giant coming toward him.

"You've built your castle in a stupid place, Prince," said the giant.

"I don't want it here," said the Prince. "It came here by accident."

"What reward will you give me for putting it back in the bundle?" asked the giant.

"What reward do you want?"

"Give me your first son, when he is seven years old," replied the giant.

"Yes, I'll do that, if I have a son," said the Prince.

In an instant, the giant put the castle, orchards and gardens back in the bundle as it was before.

"Now go your way," said the giant, "and I'll go mine. But remember your promise. If you forget, I'll remember."

The Prince set off, and after several days reached his favourite place. He opened the bundle in a fresh green hollow near his father's castle. Up sprang a castle, with orchards and gardens.

When he opened the castle door he saw a beautiful maiden.

"Everything is ready," she said, "if you are willing to marry me to-night."

"I am willing," said the Prince. And they were married that night.

When nine months had passed, a fine son was born to them. In the years that followed, the old King died and the young Prince became King in his place.

At the end of seven years and a day, the giant came to the castle. The young King remembered his promise.

"Do not worry," said the Queen, "just leave it to me. I know what to do."

Now, the giant grew impatient when he saw that the King did not have his young son with him.

"Bring out your son," said he. "Remember your promise."

"You can have him," said the King, "when his mother has made him ready for the journey."

The Queen dressed the cook's son, brought him out, and put his hand into the giant's hand. The giant led him away, but he had not gone far before he handed the boy a rod.

"If your father had that rod," said the giant, "what would he do with it?"

"He would beat the dogs and the cats if they went near the King's meat," said the lad.

"You're the cook's son!" said the giant, and returned to the castle.

"If you do not hand over your true son to me," he roared, "the highest stone of your castle will be the lowest."

"We'll try again," said the Queen to her husband. "The butler's son is the same age as ours."

She dressed the butler's son, brought him out, and put his hand into the giant's hand. They had not gone far before the giant handed the boy a rod.

"If your father had that rod, what would he do with it?"

"He'd beat the cats and dogs if they came near the King's wine-cellar."

"You are the butler's son," said the giant, and returned to the castle. The earth trembled under his feet, the castle shook and everything in it.

"Bring your son out here," he shouted, "or in a flash the highest stone in your castle will be the lowest."

So the King brought his son and gave him to the giant, who took him home and brought him up as his own son.

One day, when the giant was out, the lad heard music coming from a window at the top of the giant's house, and looking up he saw the giant's youngest daughter. She told him to come again at midnight.

He did so and the giant's daughter climbed down beside him.

"To-morrow you will be given the choice of my two sisters in marriage," said she. "Say you will take no one but me. My father wants me to marry the son of the King of the Green City, but I don't love him."

Next day the giant brought out his three daughters.

"Now, King's son," said he, "you've lost nothing by living with me so long. Now you'll marry one of my elder daughters."

"If you'll give me your youngest daughter," said the King's son, "I'll agree."

"Before you have her," said the giant, "you must do three things."

Then the giant took him to the byre.

"A hundred cattle have been in this byre, and it hasn't been cleaned for seven years," said the giant. "If, before night, the byre is not so clean that a golden apple will run from one end to the other, you'll not marry my daughter, and I'll kill you."

The Prince began to clean the byre, but he might as well have tried to bale out the ocean. After midday, when the sweat was blinding him, the giant's youngest daughter came to him.

"You are being punished, King's son," said she.

"I am that," said he.

"Come here," she said, "and lay down your weariness."

"I'll do that," said he; "there is only death awaiting me in any case."

He sat down beside her, and was so tired that he fell asleep. When he awoke, the giant's daughter was gone, and the byre was so clean that a golden apple would run from one end of it to the other.

"You've cleaned the byre, King's son," said the giant, as he came in.

"I have," said the Prince.

"Someone has cleaned it," said the giant. "Now you must thatch this byre with feathers, by this time to-morrow, and no two feathers are to be the same colour."

The Prince was up before the sun. He took his bow and quiver of arrows to shoot the birds. He ran after them till the sweat blinded him, but he missed all but two. Then the youngest daughter came to him.

"You are tiring yourself, King's son," said she.

"Only two blackbirds fell, and they are the same colour."

"Come here, and lay down your weariness," she said.

He sat down beside her and soon fell asleep. When he awoke she had gone, but the byre was thatched with feathers, and no two were the same colour.

"You've thatched the byre, King's son," said the giant, as he came in. "Now, there is a fir tree beside the loch, and on its top branches a magpie's nest with five eggs in it. Bring them to me by this time to-morrow."

The Prince was up before the sun. He went round and round the fir tree, trying to find a foothold, till he was blinded by sweat. Then the Giant's youngest daughter came to him.

"You're losing the skin off your hands," she said.

"I'm no sooner up than down," said he.

"There is no time to lose," she said, putting her fingers, one after the other, into the tree, making footholds up to the magpie's nest. He climbed the tree and took the eggs.

"Make haste!" she cried. "I feel my father's breath

burning my neck!" In her hurry she left the little finger of her right hand in the tree.

"Take the eggs to my father," she said. "To-night he'll give you the choice of his three daughters. We'll be dressed alike, but choose the one whose little finger is missing."

So the Prince gave the eggs to the giant.

"Now you can choose your wife," said he.

The giant presented his three daughters, dressed exactly alike, and the Prince chose the one whose little finger was missing. They were married, but when night came she said:

"We must fly, or my father will kill you. Go and saddle the grey filly while I play a trick on him."

She cut an apple into nine pieces. She put two pieces at the head of her bed, two at the foot of her bed, two at the door, two at the house door and one in the garden. Then they mounted the grey filly, and away they rode.

The giant awoke.

"Are you asleep?" he called.

"Not yet," said the apple at the head of the bed.

"Are you asleep?" he called, after a while.

"Not yet," said the apple at the foot of the bed.

"Are you asleep?" he called again.

"Not yet," said the apple at the door.

"Are you asleep?" called the giant later.

"Not yet," said the apple at the house door.

"You are going away!" said the giant.

"Not yet," said the apple in the garden.

At that, the giant jumped out of bed and, finding the Prince and his bride had gone, ran after them.

In the mouth of the day, the giant's daughter said her father's breath was burning her neck.

"Quickly, put your hand in the grey filly's ear," said she.

"There is a twig of blackthorn," said he.

"Throw it behind you," said she.

No sooner had he done this than there sprang up twenty miles of blackthorn wood, so thick that a weasel could not go through.

The giant came striding headlong, and fleeced his head and neck in the thorns.

"More of my daughter's tricks!" said he. "If I had my big axe and wood knife, I wouldn't be long making my way through this."

He went home for his big axe and wood knife. He was not long returning, and soon made his way through the blackthorn.

"I'll leave the axe and the wood knife here till I return," said he.

"If you leave them, we'll steal them," said a hoodie in a tree.

"Then I'll take them home," said the giant.

He went back and left them at his house.

In the heat of the day, the giant's daughter said:

"I feel my father's breath burning my neck. Put your hand in the filly's ear, and whatever you find there, throw behind you."

He found a splinter of grey stone, and threw it behind him. At once there sprang up twenty miles of grey rock, high and broad as a range of mountains. The giant came full pelt after them, but past the rock he could not go.

"My daughter's tricks are hard to bear," said he, "but if I had my lever and my big mattock, I'd make my way through this rock in no time."

There was no help for it. He had to return for his lever and mattock. But he was not long returning, and was through the rocks in no time.

"I'll just leave the tools here," said he.

"If you do, we'll steal them," said the hoodie.

"Steal them if you want to," said the giant. "There's no time to go back with them."

Meanwhile, the Prince and the giant's daughter rode on.

"I feel my father's breath burning my neck," said she. "Put your hand into the filly's ear, King's son, and whatever you find there, throw behind you."

This time he found a bladder of water. He threw it behind him, and at once there was a fresh-water loch, twenty miles in length and breadth.

The giant came on, but was running so quickly that he did not stop till he was in the middle of the loch, where he sank and did not come up.

The next day the Prince and his wife came in sight of his father's house.

"Before we go farther, go to your father and tell him about me. But don't let any man or creature kiss you. If you do, you'll forget me."

He was given a warm welcome at his father's house. He asked them not to kiss him, but before he could say more, his old greyhound jumped up and licked his mouth. After that he forgot the giant's daughter.

She sat beside a well where the Prince had left her, but he did not return. In the mouth of night, she climbed into the fork of an oak tree by the well, and lay there.

Next day a shoemaker, who lived near by, asked his wife to fetch him a jug of water. At the well she saw, in the water, the reflection of the giant's daughter and thought it was herself. She had not imagined till now that she was so beautiful, so she threw away the jug and went home.

"Where is the water?" said the shoemaker.

"You stupid old man," said she, "I've been too long your wood-and-water slave!"

"I'm thinking, wife, that you've gone crazy," said he. "Go, daughter, and fetch your father a drink."

His daughter went, and the same thing happened to her when she saw the reflection in the water. She had not imagined till then that she was so bonny and, without fetching any water, she went home.

"Where is my drink?" said the shoemaker.

"You homespun old man," said she, "do you think I'm fit to be your slave?"

The poor shoemaker thought they had lost their wits, and went himself to the well. There he saw the lass's reflection in the water. Looking up at the tree, he saw the fairest woman he had ever seen.

"You have a bonny face," said the shoemaker. "Come down, for I need you at my house."

The shoemaker knew that this was the reflection that had driven his family crazy. He took her to his house, and gave her a share of everything.

One day, three young men came to have shoes made for the Prince, who was to be married soon. They saw the giant's daughter.

"You have a bonny daughter."

"She is that," said he, "but she is no daughter of mine."

"By St Crispin," said one of them, "I'd give a hundred pounds to marry her." And his companions said the same.

"It has nothing to do with me," said the shoemaker.

"Ask her to-night," they said, "and tell us to-morrow."

The giant's daughter heard this.

"Follow them," she said. "I'll marry one of them, but tell him to bring his purse with him."

The young man returned, giving the shoemaker a hundred pounds for tocher. When they went to rest, she lay down and asked the young man for a drink of water from the jug on the table. But his hands stuck to the jug, and the jug stuck to the table, so he could not move till daylight. He went away ashamed, and did not tell his friends what had happened to him.

Next came the second man.

"See if the latch is fastened," she said.

But the latch stuck to his hands, and he could not move till daylight. He too went away, and did not tell the third man what had happened.

Then the third man came, and the same thing happened to him. His feet stuck to the ground. He could neither come nor go, and there he stayed till daybreak. That morning he went away, and did not look behind him.

"Now," said the giant's daughter, "the sporran of gold is yours, shoemaker. I don't need it. It'll help you and reward you for your kindness."

"The shoes are ready," said the shoemaker, "and I'm taking them to the castle to-day for the Prince's wedding."

"I would like to peep at the King's son," said she.

"Come with me then," said the shoemaker. "I know the servants at the castle, and you'll get a peep at the Prince."

When the Court saw this beautiful young woman, they gave her a glass of wine. As she was about to drink, a flame sprang up out of the glass, and a golden pigeon and a silver pigeon flew out of the flame. The pigeons were flying about the hall when three grains of barley fell on the floor. The silver pigeon alighted and ate them.

"When I cleaned the byre," said the golden pigeon, "you wouldn't have eaten without giving me a share."

Three other grains of barley fell. The silver pigeon alighted and ate them up.

"When I thatched the byre," said the golden pigeon, "you wouldn't have eaten without giving me a share."

Three other grains of barley fell. The silver pigeon ate them up too.

"When I harried the magpie's nest," said the golden pigeon, "you would not have eaten without giving me a share, and I lost my little claw bringing it down."

Then the King's son remembered, and kissed her from hand to mouth.

The Knight of Riddles

ONCE upon a time there was a King who married a great lady, but when her first son was born she went away. Soon after, the King married again and had a second son. The two lads grew up together.

One day the Queen realised that it was not her son who would become King, and decided to poison the elder brother. She told the cook to put poison in the lad's drink. Luckily, the younger brother overheard her and told his brother not to touch the drink. The Queen wondered why the lad was still alive. Thinking that too little poison had been used, she asked the cook to try again that night. The younger brother overheard this too, and repeated his warning.

The elder brother put the poisoned drink into a little bottle, and said:

"If I stay at home she'll kill me some way or other. The quicker I leave the house the better. I'll take the world for my pillow, and seek my fortune."

His brother decided to go with him. They went to the stable, saddled two horses, and rode away.

Not far from the house, the elder brother said:

"We don't know if the drink was poisoned or not. Try it in the horse's ear!"

The horse had not gone very far when he fell dead.

"It was only a bag of bones in any case," said the elder brother. They both got on to one horse, and rode on.

"I still can't believe that there's any poison in the drink. Let's try it on this horse!"

This they did, and they had not gone very far when the horse fell dead. They took the hide off it, to keep them warm during the coming night. When they woke in the morning they saw twelve ravens alighting on the carcass. Soon after the birds fell dead.

They took the dead ravens with them, and in the first town asked a baker to make them into a dozen pies. They took the pies with them, and went on.

At the mouth of night, twenty-four robbers came out of a wood and asked them for their purses. They said they had no purses, only a little food. The robbers began to eat the pies, but had not eaten much when they fell down dead. The brothers searched their pockets and found much gold and silver. They went on till they reached the house of the Knight of Riddles. It was in a most beautiful place, but if his house was pretty, his daughter was still prettier. Her husband would be the man who could ask her father, the Knight, a riddle he could not solve.

The two lads decided to ask him a riddle, and the younger one would act as gillie to his elder brother. When they entered the house of the Knight of Riddles, they asked him this question:

"One killed two, two killed twelve, twelve killed twenty-four, and two escaped."

They would be treated with great honour till the Knight solved the riddle. They stayed with him a long time.

One day one of the daughter's maidens came to the gillie, and asked him to tell her the answer. He took her plaid off, and let her go without telling her the answer. He did the same with all twelve maidens, one by one, as they came to him day by day. He told the last one that only his master knew the answer to the riddle. He told his elder brother everything as it happened.

One day after that, the Knight's daughter herself came to the elder brother, and asked him to tell her the answer. He could not refuse her, and told her, but kept her plaid. The Knight of Riddles sent for him, and told him the answer.

The Knight gave him two choices, either to lose his head, or to be sent away in a leaky boat without oars or baler. The lad said:

"I have another question for you, before this happens."

"Ask me!" said the Knight.

"One day, I and my gillie were shooting in the forest. He shot at a hare, and she fell. He took her skin off, and let her go. He did this to twelve hares, taking their skins off and letting them go. At last there came a large, fine hare. I myself fired at her, took her skin off, and let her go."

"Your riddle is too hard to solve," said the Knight.

So the lad married the Knight's daughter, and they made a great wedding that lasted a year and a day. The younger brother went home, now that his elder brother was getting on so well, and the elder gave the younger every claim on their father's kingdom.

Near the domain of the Knight of Riddles lived three giants, who were murdering the Knight's people, and despoiling them. The Knight said to his son-in-law, one day, that if he had the spirit of a man he would slay the giants. So he went out to meet the giants, and came home with their three heads, which he threw at the Knight's feet.

"You are an able fellow," said the Knight, "and your name from now on will be the Hero of the White Shield."

The Hero of the White Shield's name went far and wide.

The Hero of the White Shield's brother was very strong and clever. He did not know that the Hero was his brother, and proposed to play a trick on him. The Hero was now living in the land of the giants, and the Knight's daughter with him. His brother challenged him to wrestle. They wrestled from morning till evening. Then, when they were tired and weak, the Hero of the White Shield jumped over the rampart, and asked him to meet him in the morning. The leap put his brother to shame, and he said:

"I hope you will be as supple this time to-morrow."

The younger brother slept that night in a little bothy near the Hero of the White Shield's house, and in the morning they began to wrestle again. The Hero was pushed back, till he went into the river.

"There must be some of my blood in you, when you have done that to me," he said.

"Of what blood are you?" asked the younger brother.

"I am son of Ardan, King of the Albann."

"Then I am your brother."

Now they recognised and welcomed each other. The Hero of the White Shield took his brother into the palace, and the Knight's daughter was pleased to see him. He stayed for a time with them, and then he thought he would go home to his own kingdom. As he was going past a great palace there, he saw twelve men playing at shinty near the palace. He went to play shinty with them, but soon they quarrelled. The weakest of them caught him, and shook him like a child. He knew it was useless to lift a hand among these twelve worthies, and asked them who their father was. They said they were all sons of one father, the Hero of the White Shield's brother, but no two of them had the same mother.

"I am your father," he said, and asked them if their mothers were all alive. They said that they were. He went with them to meet their mothers, and when they all agreed to go he took the twelve wives and their twelve sons home with him. Maybe his descendants still rule in Alba.

The Good Housewife

[ARGYLLSHIRE]

ONE night, long after her husband and family were in bed, a rich farmer's wife was finishing some cloth.

"Oh that I had some help with this cloth!" she said aloud. At once there was a knock at the door.

"Inary, good housewife, open the door and I'll share with you all I have."

A strange woman in green came in, and sat down at the spinning-wheel. There was a second knock at the door.

"Inary, good housewife, open the door and I'll share with you all I have."

Another strange woman in green came in, and sat down at the distaff. There was a third knock at the door.

"Inary, good housewife, open the door and I'll share with you all I have."

Another strange woman in green came in, and sat down to card the wool. There was a fourth knock at the door.

63

"Inary, good housewife, open the door and I'll share with you all I have."

Another strange woman in green came in, and sat down to tease the wool. There was a fifth knock at the door.

"Inary, good housewife, open the door and I'll share with you all I have."

Another strange woman in green came in, and sat down to pull the wool. A sixth and a seventh and an eighth and a ninth and a tenth, and many more weird women and men came in, and went to work with distaff, cards, spinning-wheel and loom. The house was full of fairies, teasing, carding, pulling and rolling. The fulling water was boiling over.

Among the whirr and rasp and rustle and thrum, the good housewife prepared a meal for them. But the more they worked the hungrier they grew, till the sweat dripped off the goodwife's face.

At midnight she tried to waken the goodman, but he slept like a millstone. Then she thought of a wise man she knew. Leaving the fairies eating her new loaves, she slipped out of the house.

"As long as you live," said the wise man, "don't wish for anything unwise, in case your wish is answered and brings you evil. Your husband is under a spell, and before you can waken him your visitors must leave the house, and you must sprinkle some fulling water over the goodman."

"How can I rid myself of my strange visitors?" she asked.

"Return home!" said the wise man, "stand on the knowe at your door, and shout three times, 'Burg Hill's on fire!' The fairies will rush out to look. While they are outside, invert, reverse, put everything topsy-turvy, mixter-maxter."

She went home and climbed the knowe at her door.

"Burg Hill's on fire! Burg Hill's on fire! Burg Hill's on fire!" she shouted.

The fairy people rushed out of the house, crying for the treasures they had left in the fairy mound. The goodwife shut the door and fastened it. Then she took the band off the spinning-wheel, spun the distaff the wrong way, put the wool-cards together, turned the loom mixty-maxty and took the fulling water off the fire.

"Inary, good housewife, let us in!" begged the fairies.

"I can't," said the goodwife. "I'm baking bread."

"Spinning-wheel, come and open the door!" they said.

"I can't," said the spinning-wheel. "I have no band."

"Distaff, come and open the door!" they said.

"I can't. I'm twisted the wrong way."

"Wool-cards, come and open the door!"

"We can't move," said the cards.

"Loom, come and open the door!"

"I can't. I'm all mixter-maxter."

"Fulling water, come and open the door!"

"I can't. I'm off the fire."

They remembered the little Bannock that was toasting on the hearth.

"Little Bannock," they said, "open the door!"

The little Bannock jumped up, and ran to the door. But the goodwife was too quick for him. She caught him and he fell on the floor, broken.

Then the goodwife remembered what she had to do with the fulling water. She threw a cogful over the goodman, who woke up at once. He got out of bed, and opened the door. The fairies became quiet and went away.

The King of Lochlin's Three Daughters

[ARGYLLSHIRE]

THERE was a King of Lochlin, who had three daughters. One day when they were out for a walk they were carried off by three giants, and no one knew where they had gone. The King consulted a Sheanachaidh, and the wise man told him that the giants had taken them under the earth.

"The only way to reach them," said he, "is to build a ship that will sail on land and sea."

So the King sent out a proclamation that any man who could make such a ship could marry his eldest daughter.

Now there was a widow who had three sons. The eldest went to his mother and said:

"Bake me a bannock and roast me a cock. I am going to cut wood and build a ship to sail on land and sea."

"A large bannock with a curse, or a small bannock with a blessing?" asked his mother.

"A large bannock will be small enough before I've built the ship!"

Away he went, with his bannock, to a wood by the river. He sat down to eat, when a great Uruisg came up out of the water.

"Give me a share of your bannock," said she.

"I'll not do that," said he. "There's little enough for myself."

After he had eaten, he began to chop down the trees, but as soon as he felled a tree it was standing and growing again. At night he gave up and went home.

The next day the second son asked his mother to bake him a bannock and roast him a cock.

"A large bannock with a curse, or a small bannock with a blessing?" she asked.

"A large one will be little enough!" said he.

Away he went, with his bannock, to the wood by the river. He sat down to eat, when a great Uruisg came up out of the water.

"Give me a share of your bannock," said she.

"There is less than enough for myself," he replied.

The same thing happened to him as to his eldest brother. As fast as he cut down a tree, so it would be standing again. So he gave up and went home.

Next day the youngest son asked his mother to bake him a bannock and roast him a cock. But he chose the wee bannock with a blessing.

Away he went to the wood by the river. There he sat down to eat, when a great Uruisg came up out of the water, and said:

"Give me a share of your bannock."

"You shall have that," said the lad, "and some of the roasted cock too, if you like."

After the Uruisg had eaten, she said:

"Meet me here at the end of a year and a day, and I shall have a ship ready to sail on land and sea."

"I'll do that," said the lad, and returned home.

At the end of a year and a day, the youngest son found that the Uruisg had the ship ready. He went aboard, and sailed away.

He had not sailed far when he saw a man drinking up a river.

"Come with me," said the lad. "I'll give you meat and wages, and better work than that."

"Agreed!" said the man.

They had not sailed far when they saw a man eating all the oxen in a field.

"Come with me," said the lad. "I'll give you meat and wages, and better work than that."

"Agreed!" said the man.

They had not sailed much farther when they saw a man with his ear to the ground.

"What are you doing?" asked the lad.

"I'm listening to the grass coming up through the earth," said the man.

"Come with me," said the lad. "I'll give you meat, wages and better work than that."

So he went with the lad and the other two men, and they sailed on till the Listener said:

"I hear the giants and the King's three daughters under the earth."

So they let a creel down the hole, with the four of them in it, to the dwelling of the first giant and the King's eldest daughter.

"You've come for the King's daughter," said the giant, "but you'll not get her unless you have a man that can drink as much water as I."

The lad set the Drinker to compete with the giant. Before the Drinker was half full, the giant burst. They freed the eldest daughter, and went to the house of the second giant.

"You've come for the King's daughter," said he, "but you'll not get her till you find a man who can eat as much as I."

So the lad set the Eater to compete with the giant. Before he was half full, the giant burst. They freed the second daughter, and went to the house of the third giant.

"You've come for the King's daughter," said the giant, "but you'll not get her unless you are my slave for a year and a day."

"Agreed!" said the lad.

Then he sent the three men up in the creel, and after them the three Princesses. The three men led them back to the King of Lochlin, and took all the credit. So the King agreed that they should marry his daughters, while the lad was the giant's slave.

At the end of a year and a day the giant said:

"I have an eagle that will carry you to the top of the hole."

The lad mounted the eagle's back, taking five and ten oxen to feed the eagle, but they were eaten before the eagle had flown half way. So they returned.

"You'll be my slave for another year and a day," said the giant.

At the end of that time the lad mounted the eagle's back, taking ten and twenty oxen to feed the eagle, but they were eaten before the eagle had flown three-quarters of the way. So they returned.

"You must be my slave for another year and a day," said the giant.

At the end of that time the lad mounted the eagle's back, taking three score of oxen to feed the eagle on the way, and they had just reached the top when the meat was finished. Quickly the lad cut a piece from his own thigh and gave it to the eagle. With one breath they were in the open air.

Before she left him, the eagle gave the lad a whistle.

"If you are in difficulty," said she, "whistle, and I'll help you."

When the lad reached the King of Lochlin's castle, he went to the smith and asked him if he needed a gillie to blow the bellows. The smith agreed to take him.

Shortly after, the King's eldest daughter ordered the smith to make her a golden crown, like the one she had worn under the earth.

"Bring me the gold, and I'll make the crown," said the new gillie.

The smith brought the gold. Then the gillie whistled, and the eagle came at once.

"Fetch the golden crown that hangs behind the first giant's door!"

The eagle returned with the crown, which the smith took to the King's eldest daughter.

"This looks like the crown I had before," said she.

Then the second daughter ordered the smith to make her a silver crown like the one she had worn under the earth.

"Bring me the silver, and I'll make the crown," said the gillie.

The smith brought the silver. Then the gillie whistled, and the eagle came at once.

"Fetch the silver crown that hangs behind the second giant's door," said the lad.

The eagle returned with the crown, which the smith took to the King's daughter.

"This looks like the crown I had before," said she.

Then the King's youngest daughter ordered the smith to make her a copper crown like the one she had worn under the earth.

"Bring me the copper, and I'll make the crown," said the gillie.

The smith brought the copper. Then the gillie whistled, and the eagle came at once.

"Fetch the copper crown that hangs behind the third giant's door," said the gillie.

The eagle returned with the crown, which the smith took to the King's youngest daughter.

"This looks like the crown I had before," said she.

"Where did you learn to make such fine crowns?" the King asked the smith.

"It was my gillie who made them," said he.

"I must see him," said the King, "and ask him to make me a crown."

The King sent a coach-and-four to fetch the gillie from the smiddy, but when the coachmen saw how dirty he looked they threw him into the coach like a dog. So he whistled for the eagle, who came at once.

"Get me out of this," said he, "and fill the coach with stones."

The King came to meet the coach. When the coachmen opened the door for the gillie, the stones tumbled out instead.

Other servants were sent to fetch the gillie, but they treated him just as badly, so he whistled for the eagle.

"Get me out of this," said he, "and fill the coach with rubbish from the midden."

Again the King came to meet the coach, but when the door was opened for the gillie, a great heap of rubbish fell out on the King.

The King then sent his trusted old servant to fetch the gillie. He went straight to the smiddy, and found the lad blowing the bellows, his face black with soot.

"The King wishes to see you," said he, "but first, clean a little of the soot off your face."

The lad washed himself and went with the servant to the King. On the way he whistled for the eagle.

"Fetch me the gold and silver clothes belonging to the giants," said he.

The eagle returned with the clothes, and when the lad put them on, he looked like a Prince.

The King came to meet him, and took him to the castle, where he was told the whole story from beginning to end.

The Drinker, the Eater and the Listener, who were to have married the Princesses, were punished. The King gave his eldest daughter to the lad, so they were married, and the wedding lasted twenty days and twenty nights.

The Wife and her Bush of Berries

[LOWLAND]

ONCE upon a time there was a wife who lived in a house by herself. As she was sweeping the house one day, she found twelve pennies.

She wondered what she would do with her twelve pennies, and at last thought she couldn't do better than go to the market. So she went to the market, and bought a kid.

As she was going home she spied a bonny bush of berries growing beside a bridge.

"Kid, kid," said she, "look after my house till I pull my bonny, bonny bush of berries."

"Indeed not," said the kid, "I'll not look after your house till you pull your bonny bush of berries."

Then the wife went to the dog, and said:

"Dog, dog, bite kid!
Kid won't look after my house,
While I pull my bonny, bonny bush of berries."

"Indeed," said the dog, "I'll not bite the kid, for the kid never did me any harm."

72

Then the wife went to the staff, and said:

> *"Staff, staff, beat dog!*
> *Dog won't bite kid;*
> *Kid won't look after my house,*
> *While I pull my bonny, bonny bush of berries."*

"Indeed," said the staff, "I won't beat the dog, for the dog never did me any harm."

Then the wife went to the fire, and said:

> *"Fire, fire, burn staff!*
> *Staff won't beat dog;*
> *Dog won't bite kid;*
> *Kid won't look after my house,*
> *Till I pull my bonny, bonny bush of berries."*

"Indeed," said the fire, "I won't burn the staff, for the staff never did me any harm."

Then the wife went to the water, and said:

> *"Water, water, quench fire!*
> *Fire won't burn staff;*
> *Staff won't beat dog;*
> *Dog won't bite kid;*
> *Kid won't look after my house,*
> *Till I pull my bonny, bonny bush of berries."*

"Indeed," said the water, "I will not quench the fire, for the fire never did me any harm."

Then the wife went to the ox, and said:

> *"Ox, ox, drink water!*
> *Water won't quench fire;*
> *Fire won't burn staff;*

> *Staff won't beat dog;*
> *Dog won't bite kid;*
> *Kid won't look after my house,*
> *Till I pull my bonny, bonny bush of berries."*

"Indeed," said the ox, "I won't drink the water, for the water never did me any harm."

Then the wife went to the axe, and said:

> *"Axe, axe, fell ox!*
> *Ox won't drink water;*
> *Water won't quench fire;*
> *Fire won't burn staff;*
> *Staff won't beat dog;*
> *Dog won't bite kid;*
> *Kid won't look after my house,*
> *Till I pull my bonny, bonny bush of berries."*

"Indeed," said the axe, "I won't fell the ox, for the ox never did me any harm."

Then the wife went to the smith, and said:

> *"Smith, smith, blunt axe!*
> *Axe won't fell ox;*
> *Ox won't drink water;*
> *Water won't quench fire;*
> *Fire won't burn staff;*
> *Staff won't beat dog;*
> *Dog won't bite kid;*
> *Kid won't look after my house,*
> *Till I pull my bonny, bonny bush of berries."*

"Indeed," said the smith, "I won't blunt the axe, for the axe never did me any harm."

Then the wife went to the rope, and said:

> *"Rope, rope, hang smith!*
> *Smith won't blunt axe;*
> *Axe won't fell ox;*
> *Ox won't drink water;*
> *Water won't quench fire;*
> *Fire won't burn staff;*
> *Staff won't beat dog;*
> *Dog won't bite kid;*
> *Kid won't look after my house,*
> *Till I pull my bonny, bonny bush of berries."*

"Indeed," said the rope, "I won't hang the smith, for the smith never did me any harm."

Then the wife went to the mouse, and said:

> *"Mouse, mouse, cut rope!*
> *Rope won't hang smith;*
> *Smith won't blunt axe;*
> *Axe won't fell ox;*
> *Ox won't drink water;*
> *Water won't quench fire;*
> *Fire won't burn staff;*
> *Staff won't beat dog;*
> *Dog won't bite kid;*
> *Kid won't look after my house,*
> *Till I pull my bonny, bonny bush of berries."*

"Indeed," said the mouse, "I won't cut the rope, for the rope never did me any harm."

Then the wife went to the cat, and said:

> *"Cat, cat, kill mouse!*
> *Mouse won't cut rope;*
> *Rope won't hang smith;*

Smith won't blunt axe;
Axe won't fell ox;
Ox won't drink water;
Water won't quench fire;
Fire won't burn staff;
Staff won't beat dog;
Dog won't bite kid;
Kid won't look after my house,
Till I pull my bonny, bonny bush of berries."

"Indeed," said the cat, "I won't eat the mouse, for the mouse never did me any harm."

"Do it," said the wife, "and I'll give you a dish of cream."

With that, the cat began to kill the mouse,
The mouse began to cut the rope,
The rope began to hang the smith,
The smith began to blunt the axe,
The axe began to fell the ox,
The ox began to drink the water,
The water began to quench the fire,
The fire began to burn the staff,
The staff began to beat the dog,
The dog began to bite the kid,
And the kid looked after the wife's house,
Till she pulled her bonny, bonny bush of berries.

Finn and the Young Hero's Children

ONE day Finn and his men were hunting on the hill. They had killed many deer and sat in the sun out of the wind. They could see everyone and nobody could see them.

Finn saw a ship making straight for the haven beneath them. A Young Hero leaped out of her, and pulled the ship on to the green grass. Then he climbed the hill to Finn and his men.

Finn and he greeted each other, and Finn asked him where he had come from and what he wanted. He answered that he had come through the night watches and storms of the sea, because he was losing his children and only one man could help him. That man was Finn, King of the Feinne.

"I lay a spell on you," said he to Finn, "to be with me before you eat, drink or sleep."

Having said this, he left them. When he reached the ship, he pushed her, with his shoulder, into the water. Then he leaped into her, and sailed away over the horizon.

Finn said good-bye to his men, and went down to the shore. He walked along it, and saw seven men coming to meet him.

"What are you good at?" he asked the first man.

"I am a good carpenter."

"How good are you at carpentry?"

"With three strokes of my axe I can make a ship of the alder tree yonder."

"What are you good at?" he asked the second man.

"I am a good tracker."

"How good are you?"

77

"I can track the wild duck over the nine waves within nine days."

"What are you good at?" he asked the third man.

"I am a good gripper."

"How good are you?"

"I will not let go till my two arms part from my shoulders, or till what I hold comes with me."

"What are you good at?" he asked the fourth man.

"I am a good climber. I can climb a thread of silk to the stars, if you tie it there."

"What are you good at?" he asked the fifth man.

"I am a good thief. I can steal the heron's egg while she is watching me."

"What are you good at?" he asked the sixth man.

"I am a good listener. I can hear what people are saying at the end of the world."

"What are you good at?" he asked the seventh man.

"I am a good marksman. I could hit an egg in the sky as far away as bowstring and bow can carry the arrow."

The Carpenter went to the alder tree, and with three strokes of his axe the ship was ready. Finn ordered his men to push her into the water, and they went on board.

The Tracker went to the bow. Finn told him how the Young Hero had left the haven in his ship, and Finn wanted to follow him to the place where he now was. The Tracker told him to keep the ship that way or to keep her this way. They sailed a long time without seeing land, till the evening. In the gloaming they saw land ahead, and made straight for it. They leaped ashore and drew up the ship.

They walked toward a large house in the glen above the beach. As they came near it the Young Hero came to meet them.

"Dearest of all men in the world, have you come?" he said, and threw his arms about Finn's neck.

In the house, after their hunger and thirst were satisfied, the Young Hero told his story:

"Six years ago, my wife had a baby. But a large hand came down the chimney and took the child away. Three years ago, the same thing happened. To-night my wife is going to have another baby, and I have been told you are the only man in the world who can keep my children for me."

Finn told his men to stretch themselves on the floor, and he would keep watch. He sat beside the fire. He had an iron bar in the fire, and when his eyes began to close he pushed the bar against his palm to keep himself awake.

About midnight the baby was born, and immediately the Hand came down the chimney. Finn called the Gripper, who sprang to his feet and grasped the Hand, pulling the Giant in as far as the eyebrows. The Hand pulled the Gripper out as far as the top of his shoulders. The Gripper pulled the Hand again, and brought it in as far as the neck. The Hand pulled the Gripper, and brought him out as far as his waist. The Gripper pulled the Hand, and brought it in as far as the two armpits. The Hand pulled the Gripper, and brought him out as far as the soles of his two feet. Then the Gripper gave a great pull on the Hand, and it came out of the shoulder. When it fell on the floor the pull of seven horses was in it. But the big Giant put his other hand down the chimney, and took the child away.

They were all very sorry for the loss of the child. But Finn said, "We will not give in. I and my men will go after the Hand before sunrise."

At dawn, Finn and his men launched the ship. The Tracker went to the bow, and Finn steered. The Tracker told Finn to keep her in that direction, or to keep her in this direction. They sailed far without seeing anything but the ocean. At sunset there was a black spot in the sea ahead. Finn thought it was too small for an island and too big for a bird, but he steered toward it. At dusk they reached it, and it was a rock. On top of it was a castle thatched with eelskins.

They landed on the rock, but the castle had neither window nor door, except on the roof, and the thatch was slippery.

"I'll not be long in climbing it," cried the Climber. He sprang toward the castle, and in a moment was on the roof. He looked in, took note of everything he saw, and slid down where the others were waiting.

"What did you see?" Finn asked.

"I saw a big Giant lying on a bed, a silk covering over him, and a satin sheet under him. An infant slept in his outstretched hand. Two boys were playing shinty on the floor with sticks of gold and a silver ball. A very large deer-hound was lying beside the fire nursing her two pups."

"I don't know how we'll bring them out," said Finn.

"I'll not be long in fetching them out," said the Thief.

"Come on to my back and I'll take you to the door," said the Climber. The Thief did so, and went into the castle.

He fetched the child from the Giant's hand, the two boys who were playing, the silk covering from over the Giant, and the satin sheet from under him. Then he fetched the sticks of gold and the silver ball, and the two pups from their mother. There was nothing else of value, so he left the Giant sleeping and came out.

They put everything into the ship and sailed away. Soon after that the Listener stood up.

"I hear him," he said.

"What do you hear?" said Finn.

"He has just wakened," said the Listener, "and missed everything we stole. He is very angry. He's sending the deer-hound. He's telling her that if she won't go he'll go himself. It's the hound that's coming."

Soon behind them they saw the hound coming. She was

swimming so fast, red sparks were coming from her. They were afraid.

"Throw out one of the pups," said Finn. "Maybe when she sees the pup drowning, she'll go back with it." They threw out the pup, and she went back with it.

Soon after the Listener stood up, trembling.

"I hear him," he said.

"What do you hear now?" said Finn.

"He's sending the hound again. But as she won't go, he's coming himself."

After they heard this, their eyes were always behind them. At last they saw him coming, and the ocean rose no farther than his thighs. They were terribly afraid, and didn't know what to do. But Finn thought of his wisdom tooth, and put his finger under it. He learned that the Giant was immortal, except for a mole on his palm.

"If I catch one glimpse of it, I'll have him," said the Marksman.

The Giant waded through the sea to the side of the ship. He put up his hand to seize the top of the mast, to sink the ship. But when his hand was up, the Marksman saw the mole and let fly an arrow which hit the spot, and the Giant fell dead into the sea.

They turned about, and sailed back to the castle. The Thief again stole the pup, and they took it along with the one they had. They returned to the Young Hero. In the haven they leaped ashore, and pulled the ship on to dry land.

Then Finn went to the Young Hero's house, taking with him the Young Hero's family and everything he and his men had taken out of the Giant's castle.

The Young Hero met him, and when he saw his children he kneeled before Finn.

"What reward do you want?" he said.

"I ask for nothing but my choice of the two pups we took from the castle."

This pup was Bran, and his brother that the Young Hero got was the Grey Dog.

The Young Hero took Finn and his men into his house, and made a merry feast which lasted for a year and a day, and if the last day was not the best, it was not the worst.

The Stove Worm

THE length of the master Stove Worm was beyond telling, and reached thousands and thousands of miles in the sea.

His tongue itself was hundreds and hundreds of miles long, and with it he would sweep whole towns, trees and hills into the sea. It was forked, and the prongs he used to seize his prey. With it he would crush the largest ship like an egg-shell. With it he would crack the walls of the biggest castle like a nut and suck every living thing out of it.

One time the master Stove Worm set up his head near the shore, and the folk had to feed him, every Saturday morning, with seven young maidens.

The people went to an old speyman for advice, and he said that, if the King's daughter were given to the Stove Worm, the monster would leave and trouble them no more. The King was very sad, for the Princess was his only child and heir. Nevertheless he had to agree. But first he insisted on having ten weeks' grace. He used the time to send to the countries around, offering his daughter and kingdom to any man who would destroy the Stove Worm.

On the last day of the ten weeks the Master Assipattle made his appearance. In his boat he entered the Serpent's mouth, rowed down through the monster's gullet, set fire to the Stove Worm's liver, and returned to land.

The liver, being full of oil, blazed into a terrible fire, and the heat caused the Stove Worm great pain, so that he almost capsized the world by his struggles.

He flung out his tongue and raised it far in the heavens. By chance he caught hold of the moon, and they say he shifted it in the sky. He took hold of one of its horns, but by good fortune his tongue slipped over the horn. Down fell the tongue and made the earth quake.

Where it fell, the tongue formed a great channel in the face of the earth, now filled with the sea, dividing Denmark from Norway and Sweden. And they say, at the inner end of that sea are two bays made by the fork of the Stove Worm's tongue.

As the serpent lay struggling in great pain, he lifted up his head to the sky and then let it fall with violence. As he did so, he shed some of his great teeth, and they became the Orkney Isles.

The second time he did this more teeth fell out, and they became the Shetland Isles.

While in his death throes, he coiled himself into one vast lump, threw up his head, and again it fell, striking, as it always did, the bottom of the sea. This time the teeth that were knocked out became the Faroe Isles.

Then the Stove Worm rolled himself up, and his huge body, when he died, became the large island of Iceland. But his liver still burns, and the flames of its fire are sometimes seen rising from the mountains of that cold land.

Childe Rowland to the Dark Tower Came

[MORAYSHIRE]

KING ARTHUR'S sons, and their sister Burd Ellen, were playing at the ball. Childe Rowland kicked it, caught it with his knee, and sent it over the kirk. Burd Ellen went to look for the ball and did not come back. Her eldest brother went to the Warlock Merlin.

"Do you know where my sister, Burd Ellen, is?"

"Burd Ellen," said Merlin, "was carried away by the fairies. She is now in the King of Elfland's castle."

"If it is possible to bring her back," said her brother, "I'll do it, or die."

"It is possible," said Merlin, "but woe to him who tries it if he is not clear beforehand what to do."

Burd Ellen's brother made up his mind to try the adventure. Merlin trained him, and he set out. But he failed to carry out Merlin's instructions, and was heard of no more.

The second brother set out in the same way. But he failed to carry out Merlin's instructions, and was heard of no more.

Childe Rowland, the youngest brother, got the Queen's consent to look for his sister. He took his father's good sword, that never struck in vain, and went to Merlin's cave. The Warlock gave him all necessary instructions for his journey, and chiefly that he must kill everybody he met after entering Elfland. Also, he must not eat or drink anything offered him in that country, no matter how hungry or thirsty he might be, or he would never again see middle earth.

Childe Rowland set out, and travelled on and farther on, till he came to a field where the King of Elfland's horse-herd was feeding the King's horses.

"Tell me," said Childe Rowland, "where is the King of Elfland's castle?"

"I can't tell you," said the horse-herd, "but go on a little farther, and you'll come to the cowherd. Maybe he can tell you."

Childe Rowland drew the good sword that never struck in vain, and cut off the horse-herd's head.

He went on a little farther till he met the King of Elfland's cowherd, tending the King's cows.

"Tell me," said Childe Rowland, "where is the King of Elfland's castle?"

"I can't tell you," said the cowherd, "but go on a little farther, and you'll come to the shepherd. Maybe he can tell you."

Childe Rowland drew the good sword that never struck in vain, and cut off the cowherd's head.

He went on a little farther, till he met the King of Elfland's shepherd, tending the King's sheep.

"Tell me, where is the King of Elfland's castle?"

"I can't tell you," said the shepherd, "but go a little

farther, and you'll come to the goat-herd. Maybe he can tell you."

Childe Rowland drew the good sword that never struck in vain, and cut off the shepherd's head.

He went on a little farther, till he met the King of Elfland's goat-herd, tending the King's goats.

"Tell me, where is the King's castle?"

"I can't tell you," said the goat-herd, "but go on a little farther, till you come to the swineherd. Maybe he can tell you."

Childe Rowland drew the good sword that never struck in vain, and cut off the goat-herd's head.

He went on a little farther, till he met the King of Elfland's swineherd, feeding the King's swine.

"Tell me, where is the King's castle?"

"I can't tell you," said the swineherd, "but go on a little farther, till you come to the hen-wife. Maybe she can tell you."

Childe Rowland drew the good sword that never struck in vain, and cut off the swineherd's head.

He went on a little farther, till he met the King of Elfland's hen-wife, feeding the King's hens.

"Tell me, where is the King's castle?"

"Go on a little farther," said the hen-wife, "till you come to a round green hill surrounded by rings from the bottom to the top. Go round it three times widdershins, and every time say, 'Open, door! Open, door! and let me come in!' The third time, the door will open, and you may go in."

Childe Rowland drew the good sword that never struck in vain, and cut off the hen-wife's head.

He went three times widdershins round the green hill, crying, "Open, door! Open, door! and let me come in!" The third time, the door opened, and he went in. The door closed behind him.

He went through a long passage, where the air was warm.

There were neither windows nor candles, and the half-light came from the walls and roof.

He came to two wide and high folding doors, standing ajar. He entered a great hall, rich and brilliant, extending the whole length and height of the hill.

From the middle of the roof was hung, by a gold chain, an immense lamp of one hollow translucent pearl, in the centre of which was suspended a great carbuncle, that by the power of magic turned round and shed over the hall a clear and gentle light like the setting sun.

At the farther end of the hall, under a canopy, and seated on a sofa of velvet, silk and gold, combing her yellow hair with a silver comb, sat his sister Burd Ellen.

Under the power of a magic she could not resist, Burd Ellen brought him a bowl of bread and milk. But he remembered Merlin's warnings.

"I will neither taste nor touch, till I have set you free."

The folding doors opened, and the King of Elfland came in,

> With "*Fi, fi, fo, and fum!*
> *I smell the blood of a Christian man!*
> *Be he dead, be he living, with my brand*
> *I'll clash his brains from his brain-pan!*"

"Strike then, Bogle, if you dare!" said Childe Rowland. He drew his good sword that never struck in vain.

In the fight that followed, the King of Elfland was struck to the ground. Childe Rowland spared him, but the King of Elfland had to give back his sister, Burd Ellen, and his two brothers, who lay in a trance in the corner of the hall. The King of Elfland brought a small crystal phial holding a bright red liquor. With it he anointed the lips, nostrils, eyelids, ears and finger-tips of the two young men, who at once woke up.

The four of them returned home.

Jock and his Bagpipes

[FIFE]

THERE was a lad called Jock, and one day he said to his mother:

"Mother, I'm going away to seek my fortune."

"Very well, my son," said she. "Take the sieve and the dish to the well. Fetch home some water, and I'll make you a bannock. If you fetch home a lot of water, you'll get a large bannock, but if you fetch home little water, you'll get a wee one."

So he took the sieve and the dish, and went to the well. When he came to the well, he saw a wee bird sitting on the hillside, and when it saw Jock with the sieve and the dish, it said:

> *"Stuff it with moss,*
> *And clog it with clay,*
> *And that will carry*
> *The water away."*

"Oh, you stupid creature!" said Jock. "Do you think I'm going to do as you bid me? Na, na!"

So the water ran out of the sieve, and he took home a little water in the dish. His mother baked a wee bannock to him, and he went away to seek his fortune.

After he had been on the road a short while, the wee bird came to him.

"Give me a piece of your bannock," it said, "and I'll give you a feather out of my wing to make bagpipes for yourself."

"I'll not," said Jock. "It's all your fault I've such a wee bannock, and it's not enough for myself."

So the bird flew away. Jock went far, and far, and farther

than I can say. When he came to the King's house, he went in and asked for work.

"What can you do?" said the Housekeepers.

"I can sweep a house, take out ashes, wash dishes and keep cows," said he.

"Can you keep hares?"

"I don't know," said he, "but I'll try."

They told him that if he kept the hares, and brought them all home at night, he could wed the King's daughter. If he did not fetch them all home, he would be hanged.

So, in the morning, Jock set out with four and twenty hares and one cripple. He was very hungry, for he had only had a wee bannock, so he caught the crippled hare, killed it, roasted it and ate it. When the other hares saw this, they all ran away.

When he came home at night without any hares, the King was very angry, and ordered him to be hanged.

Now, his mother had another son, and he was also called Jock.

"Mother," said he, one day, "I'm going away to seek my fortune."

"Very well, son," said she. "Take the sieve and the dish to the well, and fetch home some water. If you fetch home a lot of water, you shall have a large bannock. If you fetch home little water, you'll get a wee one."

So he took the sieve and the dish, and went to the well. And there he saw a wee bird sitting on the hillside. When it saw Jock with the sieve and the dish, it said:

> *"Stuff it with moss,*
> *And clog it with clay,*
> *And that will carry*
> *The water away."*

"Ay, my bonny bird," said Jock, "I will."

So he stuffed the sieve with moss and clogged it with clay,

and was able to fetch home a lot of water. His mother baked him a very large bannock, and away he went to seek his fortune.

After he was on the road a bit, the bird came to him.

"Give me a piece of your bannock," it said, "and I'll give you a feather out of my wing to make bagpipes for yourself."

"Ay, my bonny bird, I will," said he, "for it was you who helped me to get such a large bannock."

He gave the bird a piece of his bannock.

"Pull a feather out of my wing," said the bird, "and make bagpipes for yourself."

"Na, na! I'll not pull a feather, for it'll hurt you."

"Just do as I bid," said the bird.

So Jock pulled a feather out of its wing, made the bagpipes and went along the road playing a merry tune.

He went far, and far, and farther than I can tell. When he came to the King's house, he went in and asked for work.

"What can you do?" said the Housekeepers.

"I can sweep a house, take out ashes, wash the dishes and keep cows," said he.

"Can you keep hares?"

"I don't know, but I'll try," said he.

They told him if he could keep the hares, and fetch them all home at night, he would win the King's daughter, but if he did not fetch them all home, he would be hanged.

Next morning he set out with four and twenty hares and a crippled one. Jock played them such a bonny tune on his bagpipes that they all danced round him and never left his side.

That night he fetched them all home. The crippled one could not walk, so he took it up in his arms and carried it.

The King was very well pleased, and he gave him his daughter, and Jock was King when the old King died.

The Tale of the Hoodie

[ISLAY]

ONCE upon a time there was a farmer who had three daughters. One day they were waulking clothes by a river, when a hoodie came and said to the eldest:

"Will you wed me, farmer's daughter?"

"I'll not wed you," said she. "The hoodie is an ugly creature!"

The next day he came to the second daughter, and said:

"Will you wed me, farmer's daughter?"

"I'll not wed you," said she. "The hoodie is a horrid creature!"

The third day he came to the youngest daughter, and said:

"Will you marry me, farmer's daughter?"

"Yes, I will marry you," said she. "The hoodie is a bonny creature!"

So the next day they were married.

"Would you prefer me to be a hoodie by day, and a man by night; or a hoodie by night and a man by day?" he asked.

"I would rather you were a man by day, and a hoodie by night," said she.

After that he was a handsome young man by day, and a hoodie at night. Soon after their marriage he took her to his house.

At the end of nine months they had a son. One night, when everyone was in bed, there came the most beautiful music ever heard, but everyone slept and the child was taken away by the hoodie.

The young mother wept. Her husband returned in the morning, but his child had been taken away, and he did not know what to do.

At the end of nine months they had another son. Everyone kept watch. One night the music came as before, but everyone slept, and the child was taken away by the hoodie.

The young mother wept. Her husband returned in the morning, but his child had been taken away, and he did not know what to do.

At the end of nine months they had yet another son. Watch was kept. One night the music came, but everyone slept, and the child was taken away by the hoodie.

In the morning the husband returned, and took the young mother away in a coach. On the way, he said to her:

"See if you have forgotten anything."

"I've forgotten my comb," she said. And at that instant the coach in which they were travelling became a withered stick, and he flew away as the hoodie.

She followed him. When he was on a hilltop she would climb the hill to catch him; but when she reached the top of the hill he would be in the valley. And when she was down in the valley the hoodie was on another hill. Night came, and she was tired. She had nowhere to sleep. Then she saw a light in a house far away, so she went on toward the house and was there in no time.

Looking in through the window, she saw a wee lad in the house, and her heart went out to him. The woman of the house asked her to come in and rest. So the hoodie's wife lay down, and slept till dawn.

She left the house, and went from hill to hill looking for the hoodie. She saw him on a hill, but when she reached the top of the hill he was in the valley. And when she went down into the valley the hoodie was on another hill. When night came she had no place to sleep. She saw a light in a house far away, and she reached it in no time.

She went to the door and, peeping in, saw a wee lad on the floor, and her heart went out to him. The woman of the house prepared a bed for her, so the hoodie's wife lay down and slept till dawn.

She walked on all day searching for the hoodie, and when night came she reached another house.

The woman of the house welcomed her, and told her that the hoodie had just left.

"This is the last night you will see your husband," said the woman. "If you want to catch him you must be clever and not fall asleep."

She tried to keep awake, but she was fast asleep when he came. He dropped a ring on her right hand which woke her. She tried to catch him, but caught only a feather of his wing. He left the feather and flew away, and in the morning she did not know what to do.

"He has gone over the hill of poison," said the woman, "but no one can climb it without horseshoes on both hands and feet."

So the woman dressed her as a man, told her to go to the smith and learn to make horseshoes for herself. She did this, and learned so well that she made horseshoes for her hands and feet in no time.

Then she went over the hill of poison, and on to the town, only to hear that her husband was about to marry the Laird's daughter.

There was a race in the town that day, and everyone was to be at the race, except the stranger who had come over the hill of poison. The Laird's cook came to her and asked if she would take his place, and make the meal, so that he might go to the race.

The hoodie's wife said she would. She prepared the meal, and watched carefully to see where the bridegroom was sitting. Then she let the ring and the feather fall into the broth that was set before him. With the first spoonful he took up the ring, and with the second he took up the feather.

"Bring me the cook who prepared this broth," said he.

They fetched the cook, but the bridegroom shook his head when he saw him.

"That is not the real cook," said he. "I'll not marry until she is brought to me."

Then they fetched his own true wife, who had indeed prepared the broth.

He recognised her and the spell was broken. Together they returned over the hill of poison. She threw the horse-shoes behind her, and he followed her. As they went home, they took with them their three young sons from each of the three houses. From that day they lived happily ever after.

The Gael and the London Bailie's Daughter
[BENBECULA]

ONCE a young Gael fell in love with a lady he saw in a dream. He told his father about her.

"I will marry no one else," said he, "though I have to search the whole world for her."

"Go, if you must," said his father, "and I'll give you a hundred pounds to take with you. When it is spent, come home, and I'll give you another hundred."

So the lad took the hundred pounds, and went to France, to Spain, and all over the world, but he could not find her anywhere. By the time he arrived in London, he had spent his money, his clothes were worn, and he did not know what he was going to do for a night's lodging. As he wandered along the streets, he told his story to an old woman, who offered to help him.

"I am from the Highlands of Scotland, too," she said, "and I'd be pleased to give you hospitality."

She took him to her house, gave him meat and clothes, and a comfortable bed to lie on.

"Go out into the city," she said next day, "and maybe you will meet the one you seek."

He was walking along a city street when he saw a beautiful young woman at a window. He knew at once that she was the one he had seen in his dream, but he was too shabby to approach her. So he went back to the old woman and told her everything.

"That was the London Bailie's daughter. I was her nurse, so perhaps I can help you. I'll give you fine Highland clothes. When you see her out walking along the High Street, you must tread on her gown. When she turns round, speak to her."

The lad thanked her, and did this. He went out, saw the lady and set his foot on the edge of her gown. At once she turned round.

"I ask your pardon," he said, bowing.

"It was not your fault," said she, "the gown is too long. You are a stranger here. Will you not come home and dine with us?"

As they dined, he told her his story, and how he had seen her in a dream, and searched for her ever since.

"I saw you in a dream on the same night," she said.

"Will you marry me?" said he.

"Come back here in a year and a day. In this city the Bailie, my father, must put my hand in yours before we can marry."

So the lad returned to Scotland, and told his father all that had happened. When the year was nearly spent, he set off for London, and his father gave him the other hundred pounds and some good oatmeal bannocks.

On the road he met a Sassenach.

"What is your business in London?" asked the Saxon.

"When I was there last I planted lintseed in a street, and I'm going back to see how it is growing," said the lad. "If it is ripe, I'll take it with me; if not, I'll leave it."

"Well," said the Saxon, "that's a stupid thing to do. As for me, I'm going to marry the London Bailie's only daughter."

They walked on together. At last the Saxon felt hungry. He had no food with him, and there was no house near. So he turned to the lad.

"Will you give me some of your food?"

"I have only some oatcakes," said the lad, "but you're welcome to share them. If I were a gentleman like you, I'd never travel without my mother."

"What a foolish idea!" said the Saxon, but he took a bannock and ate it. Then they went on their way.

They had not gone far when it began to rain. The Gael had a rough plaid, but the Saxon had nothing.

"Lend me your plaid!" said he.

"I'll lend you part of it," said the lad, "but if I were a gentleman like you, I'd never travel without my house."

"You are indeed a fool!" said the Saxon. "My house is four storeys high, so how could I bring it with me?"

Then he wrapped one end of the Highlander's plaid about his shoulders, and on they went.

They had not gone far when they came to a river. There was no bridge over it, and the Saxon would not wet his feet.

"Will you carry me over?" he said to the lad.

"I'll do that," said he, "but if I were a gentleman like you, I'd never travel without my own bridge."

"You're certainly a silly fellow," said the Saxon. But he got on to his back for all that, and on they went. At last they came to London town.

The Saxon went to the Bailie's house.

"On the way, I met a Gael, a most stupid fellow! He was coming to London for lint he had planted a year ago. He told me I should never travel without my mother, my house and my bridge! However, he was a good-natured fool. He shared his food and his plaid, and carried me over a river."

"He would appear as wise as the man he spoke to," said the Bailie. "The lint was the maid he left in London. If her love had grown, he would take her with him. By your mother he meant the food you should have had with you, for she was your first nourishment. By your house he meant a coach, and the bridge was your saddle-horse. A gentleman should not travel without these things and then ask help from others. A smart lad that, and I would like to meet him."

Next day the Highlander visited the Bailie, and was warmly welcomed.

"I'd like to help a smart lad like you!" said the Bailie.

"I hear it is the custom in this city," said the lad, "that no man can marry unless the Bailie gives him the bride by the hand. Will you give me the hand of the lass I've come to marry?"

"I'll do that," said the Bailie.

Next day the Bailie's daughter went, disguised, to her old nurse. The Bailie, when he came, did not recognise her.

"It's an honour for you to marry such a fine lad. Give him your hand, lass," said he. He put her hand into the lad's and they were married.

The Bailie went home. He remembered he would be giving his daughter's hand that day to the Saxon gentleman. But his daughter was nowhere to be found.

"I'll lay a wager," said he, "that the Gael has got her after all."

Just then the Gael came in with the daughter. They told him all that had happened.

"I've given you my daughter by the hand, and I'm glad she has a smart young lad like you for a husband."

They had a wedding that lasted a year and a day, and lived happily ever after.

Johnnie Croy and the Mermaid
[ORKNEY]

ONE day, Johnnie Croy went to the shore to look for driftwood. The tide was out, and he walked under the crags on the west side of Sanday. From the boulders there came the sound of singing. He peeped over the rocks. A mermaid was sitting on a rock combing her hair.

Johnnie swore by the moor-stone to court her, though the wooing cost him his life. He crept behind her, sprang forward and kissed her.

She flung Johnnie on the rocks with a blow from her tail that made his spine smart. Then she went into the sea. Johnnie stood up. It was the first time anyone had laid his back to the ground. Then he found the mermaid's comb at his feet.

"Give me my comb!" she cried.

"Nay, my buddo," said Johnnie. "You'll come and bide on land with me first."

"I couldn't bear your black rain and white snow," she said. "Your sun and smoky fires would wizen me up. Come with me, and I'll make you chief of the Fin-folk."

"You can't entice me," said Johnnie. "I have a house at Volyar, with plenty of gear, cows and sheep, and you shall be mistress of it all if you come and stay with me."

But she saw the Fin-folk coming, and swam out to sea.

Johnnie went home and told the whole story to his mother, who was a wise woman.

"You're a fool to fall in love with a sea-lass," said she, "but if you want her, you must keep her comb."

One morning he was awakened by music in his room. He sat up and saw the mermaid near his bed.

"I've come for my comb," said she.

"I'll not give it to you, my bonny lass," said he, "but will you not stay with me and be my wife?"

"I'll make you a fair offer," she said. "I'll live with you here for seven years, if you swear to come with me, and all that's mine, to see my own folk at the end of that time."

Johnnie swore by the moor-stone to keep the bargain. So they were married, and as the priest prayed the mermaid stuffed her hair in her ears.

The mermaid baked the best bread and brewed the strongest ale in all the island. She kept everything in good order, and was the best spinner in the countryside. Indeed she made the best wife and the best mother too. At their home in Volyar everything went as merry as a Yuletide.

As seven years drew near their end, the family made ready for a long voyage. Johnnie was very thoughtful and said little. His wife had a far-away look on her face.

Now, on the eve of the last day of the seven years the youngest of their seven bairns was sleeping at his grandmother's house. Before midnight came she made a wire cross, which she heated on the fire and laid on the bare seat of the bairn, he screaming like a little demon.

When morning came and they were all ready, Johnnie's wife walked down to the boat. When she came to the beach, her goodman and six only of her seven bairns were in the boat. She sent the servants back for the youngest bairn. They returned, telling her that four men had tried to lift the cradle where the bairn lay, and they could not budge it one inch.

Johnnie Croy's wife ran up to the house and tried to lift the cradle, but she could not move it. She flung back the blanket and tried to lift the bairn out of its cradle. The moment she touched him a dreadful burning went through her arms, that made her draw back and scream. She went to the boat with her head hanging and the salt tears streaming from her eyes. As the boat sailed away, the folk on the shore heard her lamenting:

"Aloor, aloor! for my bonny bairn! Aloor! for my bonny boy! Aloor! that I must leave him to live and die on dry land!"

Away, far away, sailed the boat, no one knows where. Johnnie Croy, his braw young wife, and their six bairns were never seen again by mortal eye.

Oscar and the Giant

OSCAR, son of Ossian, used to play shinty with his school-fellows on the seashore. By the time Oscar was sixteen his side always won, for he had grown very big, twice as big as any lad of his own age. Twice as many lads used to play against him as for him. At last he played alone against the rest.

One day, when they were playing shinty, they saw a boat coming in. There was a giant in her, the like they had never seen before. All the lads were afraid of him, and gathered round Oscar for protection.

The giant came toward them. Only his eyes could be seen, for he was covered with green scales, and every lad he struck with his palm lay dead on the shore. Then he struck Oscar and made him dizzy. He could just rise, but he thought it best to lie still, for if he got up he would certainly be slain.

The giant seized Oscar and put him, like a trout, on the end of a branch, and sixteen of his school-fellows on top of him. Then the giant slung the branch over his shoulder and threw it, lads and all, into his boat, Oscar underneath.

Then the giant rowed for a long time, till he reached an island. He caught hold of the branch, swung it over his shoulder, Oscar underneath.

On he went till he came to a castle. He went in and put down the branch laden with boys, and called for his house-keeper. A fine big woman appeared at the door.

"I'm going to rest now, goodwife," said he. "See that you have the biggest lad cooked ready for my supper when I wake."

The woman went over to the branch, and felt all the lads.

Oscar was the biggest, but he caught her by the hand and begged her to let him be for the present.

She took the best of the others and roasted him on the fire. He was no sooner ready than the giant awoke.

"Is my supper ready?" said he.

"Here it is," said she, setting the dish before him.

"There was a bigger lad than this," said the giant. "I shall go to sleep again, and unless you have him cooked when I wake, I'll have you instead!"

So she went to Oscar, and said:

"I must take you now."

"That is not the best thing for you," said he. "Let me live, and I will think of a better idea. You are not his wife, are you?"

"Not I. He stole me seven years ago, and I dread each day that he will kill me."

"Help me," said Oscar, "and I will help you. First, put the poker in the fire, and then loose me from this branch."

The woman did this, and then loosed him. When the poker was red, Oscar took it and drove it through the green scales of the monster's head to the ground, and the woman took his sword and struck off his head. The monster was dead, the spell was broken, and all the boys lifted themselves up off the branch.

When they left the castle they took the woman with them, and as much of the giant's gold and silver as they could carry. Then they found the giant's boat and rowed back to the shore.

The Young King
[ISLAY]

SOON after the young King of Easaidh Ruadh had ascended the throne, he thought he would gamble with a Gruagach who lived near by. He went to the soothsayer.

"I have made up my mind to gamble with the Gruagach," said he.

"Oh," said the soothsayer, "are you that kind of man? Are you rash enough to gamble with the Gruagach? My advice to you is to change your mind and not go there at all."

"I won't change my mind," said the King.

"Then my advice to you is, if you win against the Gruagach, to ask as your winnings the maid with the rough skin and the cropped head."

If the sun rose early, the King rose earlier still to gamble with the Gruagach. When he arrived, the King and the Gruagach blessed each other.

"Oh, young King of Easaidh Ruadh, what has brought you here to-day? Do you want to gamble with me?"

"I do," said the young King.

They played, and the King won.

"Lift your stakes!" said the Gruagach.

"My stakes are the girl with the rough skin and cropped head behind the door."

"I have fairer women than she," said the Gruagach.

"I will take no one but her."

They went to the Gruagach's house, and the King was shown twenty young girls.

"Choose one of these!"

They came out, one after the other, and each one said:

"I am she. You are foolish not to take me with you."

But the soothsayer had advised him to take none but the last one. When the last girl came out, he said:

"That one is mine!"

He went with her, and when they were some distance from the Gruagach's house, she turned into the most beautiful woman he had ever seen. They went together to the castle.

If it was early when the sun rose, the King rose earlier still to gamble with the Gruagach.

"I must gamble with the Gruagach to-day," he said to his wife.

"He is my father," said she. "If you gamble with him, take nothing for your winnings but the shaggy filly with the wooden saddle."

The King went to meet the Gruagach.

"Well," said the Gruagach, "how did your young bride please you?"

"She pleased me very well."

"Have you come to gamble with me again to-day?"

"I have," replied the King.

They gambled and the King won.

"Lift your winnings, and be sharp about it!"

"My stake is the shaggy filly with the wooden saddle," said the King.

The Gruagach took the shaggy filly out of the stable. The King mounted her, and how swift she was! His wife welcomed him, and they were merry together that night.

"I would rather," said his young wife, "that you would not gamble with the Gruagach any more, for if he wins he will bring you trouble."

"I will play once more with him," said the King.

He went to gamble with the Gruagach, and the Gruagach looked pleased to see him. They played, and this time the Gruagach won.

"Lift your winnings," said the young King, "and don't be too hard on me."

"What you owe me is the Sword of Light that belongs to the King of the Oak Windows, otherwise the girl with the rough skin and the cropped head will kill you."

The King went home heavy-hearted. The young Queen met him as he came home.

"You have brought nothing with you to-night?"

The King sat down and drew her toward him, and his heart was so heavy that the chair broke under him.

"What is the matter?" said the Queen. The King told her what had happened.

"Do not worry," she said. "You have the best wife in Erin, and the second-best horse. You will come out of it well."

The Queen rose before dawn, and set everything in order. She groomed the shaggy filly with the wooden saddle. The King mounted, and the Queen kissed him and wished him luck.

"Take the advice of the filly, who will tell you what to do, and all will go well," said she.

The King set out on his journey. His shaggy steed would overtake the March wind before her, and the wind behind would not catch her. They came at the mouth of dusk and lateness to the castle of the King of the Oak Windows.

"This is the end of the journey," said the filly. "I will take you to the Sword of Light. The King is now at dinner and the Sword of Light is in his room. There is a knob on its end, and when you catch the sword, draw it softly out of the window. Take it without scrape or creak."

He came to the window where the sword was. He took hold of it, and it came softly as far as the point. Then it gave a screech.

"We must go now," said the filly. "The King has heard us taking the sword."

When they had gone some distance, the filly said:

"Stop now! Look behind you!"

"I see a swarm of brown horses coming," said he.

"So far we are swifter than they," said the filly.

They rode on, and when they had gone a good distance she said:

"Look now! Who is coming?"

"A swarm of black horses, and one black horse with a white face, coming madly with a man riding him."

"That's my brother, the best horse in Erin. Be ready, when he passes me, to take the head off his rider, who will look at you. The sword in your hand is the only sword capable of taking off *his* head."

As this man rode past, he turned to look. The King drew his sword and cut off his head. Thus died the King of the Oak Windows.

"Leap on the black horse," said the filly. "Gallop as fast as he will take you. I will follow!"

The King leaped on the black horse, and reached his castle before dawn.

"I must see the Gruagach to-day, to find out if my spells are broken," he told the Queen.

"The Gruagach will ask you if you have the sword, and how you got it. Say that if it had not been for the knob on its end you would not have it. He will stretch out to see the knob on the sword, and you will see a mole on the right side of his neck. Stab it with the point of the sword. The King of the Oak Windows was his brother, and the death of the two of them is in that sword."

The Queen kissed him, and he went to the Gruagach, at the same place as before.

"Did you fetch the sword?"

"I did."

"How did you get it?"

"I wouldn't have won it but for the knob on its end."

"Let me see it!"

"It was not part of the bargain to let you see it."

"How did you win it?"

"By the knob on its end!"

As the Gruagach lifted his head to look at the sword, the King saw the mole. He was quick and stabbed it with the sword. The Gruagach fell down dead.

When the young King of Easaidh Ruadh returned home, he found his guards tied back to back. His wife and his horses had vanished.

"A great giant came," said the guards, "and took away your wife and horses."

"Sleep will not come to my eyes, nor rest to my head, till I have my wife and my horses again."

Saying this, he followed the track of the horses. Dusk and lateness were coming when, by the side of the green wood, he saw a good place for a fire, and decided to pass the night there.

There the slim dog of the green wood found him. He blessed the dog, and the dog blessed him.

"Your wife and horses were here last night with the giant," said the dog.

"That is why I am here," said the King.

"You must not be without meat," said the dog.

The dog went into the wood, brought out animals for food, and they ate together.

"I have half a mind to return home," said the King. "I'm afraid I'll never find that giant."

"Don't lose heart, you'll be successful," said the dog. "But you must not go without sleep."

So the King stretched out beside the fire and fell asleep. At the end of his watch, the dog said to him:

"Wake up, young King. Eat some food to keep your strength. Remember, if you are in difficulty, call me."

They blessed each other, and the King departed. In the

time of dusk and lateness he came to a great precipice. He made a fire there, and warmed himself by it. There the falcon of the grey rock found him.

"Your wife and horses were here last night with the giant," said the falcon.

"That is why I am here," said the King.

"You must not be without meat," said the falcon.

Away she flew, and returned with three ducks and eight blackcocks. They set out the meat and ate it.

"You must not go without sleep," said the falcon.

So the King stretched out beside the fire and fell asleep. In the morning the falcon set him on his way.

"Remember, if you are in difficulty, call me!" she said.

At night the King came to a river, and a good place for a fire. There the brown otter of the river found him.

"Your wife and horses were here last night with the giant," said the otter. "Before midday to-morrow you will see your wife, but you must not be without meat."

The otter slipped into the river, and came back with three salmon. They prepared the fish and ate it.

"You must not go without sleep," said the otter.

So the King stretched out beside the fire and fell asleep till morning.

"You'll be with your wife to-night," said the otter, "and if you are in difficulty, call me!"

The King went on till he came to a rock and, at the bottom of the chasm, saw his wife and two horses. At the foot of the rock there was a good way in.

After they had greeted each other, his wife made some food for him, and hid him behind the horses.

"I smell a stranger within," said the giant, when he returned.

"It is nothing but the smell of horsedung," said she.

When the giant went to feed the horses, they attacked and nearly killed him. He was just able to crawl away.

"The horses looked like killing you," said the Queen.

"If I had had my soul in my own keeping, they would have killed me," said he.

"Where is your soul, my dear?" asked the Queen. "I will take care of it."

"It is in the bonnach stone," said the giant.

In the morning, after the giant had gone away, she decorated the bonnach stone. In the time of dusk and lateness the giant returned home. He went to feed the horses, and they attacked him again.

"Why did you decorate the bonnach stone like that?" said he.

"Because your soul is in it."

"I see that if you knew where my soul is you would give it much respect," said the giant.

"I would," said the Queen.

"My soul is not there," said he. "It is in the threshold."

Next day she decorated the threshold. When the giant returned home and went to feed the horses, they attacked him again.

"Why did you decorate the threshold like that?" said he.

"Because your soul is in it."

"I see that if you knew where my soul is you would take care of it," said the giant.

"I would," said the Queen.

"My soul is not there," said he. "There is a great flagstone under the threshold. Under the flagstone there is a ram. In the ram there is a duck. In the duck there is an egg, and in the egg is my soul."

Next day, when the giant went away, they raised the flagstone and a ram escaped.

"The slim dog of the green wood would soon bring the ram to me," said the King. At once the slim dog came with the ram in his mouth. When they opened the ram, out flew a duck.

"The falcon of the grey rock would soon bring me the duck," said the King.

At once the falcon of the grey rock came with the duck in her mouth. When they opened the duck to take out the egg, the egg fell into the deep sea.

"The brown otter of the river would soon bring the egg to me," said the King.

At once the brown otter came with the egg in her mouth. The Queen crushed the egg, and the giant, coming home late, fell down dead.

On the way home, the King and the Queen passed a night with the brown otter of the river, a night with the falcon of the grey rock, and a night with the slim dog of the green wood.

The White Pet
[ISLAY]

THERE was once a farmer who had a White Pet. Near Christmas, he decided to kill the White Pet, who heard this and ran away.

He had not gone far when he met a Bull.

"Hullo, White Pet!" said the Bull. "Where are you going?"

"I am going to seek my fortune," said the White Pet. "They were going to kill me for Christmas, so I thought I'd better run away."

"I'll go with you," said the Bull. "They were going to do the same with me."

"The bigger the party, the better the fun," said the White Pet.

They went on till they met a Dog.

"Hullo, White Pet!" said the Dog.

"Hullo, Dog!"

"Where are you going?" said the Dog.

"I'm running away. I heard they were going to kill me for Christmas."

"They were going to do the same with me," said the Dog. "I'll go with you."

"Come, then!" said the White Pet.

On they went till a Cat joined them.

"Hullo, White Pet!" said the Cat.

"Hullo, Cat!"

"Where are you going?" said the Cat.

"I'm going to seek my fortune," said the White Pet. "They were going to kill me for Christmas."

"They were talking of killing me too," said the Cat. "I'd better go with you."

"Come on then!" said the White Pet, and on they went till they met a Cock.

"Hullo, White Pet," said the Cock.

"Hullo to yourself, Cock," said the White Pet.

"Where are you going?" said the Cock.

"I'm going away," said the White Pet. "They were going to kill me for Christmas."

"They were going to kill me too," said the Cock. "I'll go with you."

"Come on then!" said the White Pet.

They went on till they met a Goose.

"Hullo, White Pet!" said the Goose.

"Hullo yourself, Goose!" said the White Pet.

"Where are you going?" said the Goose.

"Oh," said the White Pet, "I'm running away. They were going to kill me for Christmas."

"They were going to do the same with me," said the Goose. "I'll go with you."

On they went till dark. They saw a little light far away. It came from a house, and though far off, they were not long getting there. They looked in at the window, and saw thieves counting money.

"Let each one of us call his own call," said the White Pet. "I'll call my own call. Let the Bull call his own call, the Dog his own call, the Cat her own call, the Cock his own call, and the Goose her own call."

With that they gave one loud shout:

"Gaire!"

When the thieves heard the noise, they fled into the wood near by. When the White Pet and his companions saw the house was empty, they went in. They divided the money among themselves, and then decided to go to sleep.

"Where will you sleep to-night, Bull?" said the White Pet.

"I'll sleep behind the door," said the Bull. "Where will you sleep yourself, White Pet?"

"I'll sleep in the middle of the floor," said the White Pet.

"I'll sleep beside the fire," said the Dog. "Where will you sleep, Cat?"

"I'll sleep in the candle-press," said the Cat.

"Where will you sleep, Cock?" said the White Pet.

"I'll sleep on the rafters," said the Cock. "Where will you sleep, Goose?"

"I'll sleep in the midden," said the Goose.

After they had all gone to rest, one of the thieves returned to the house and looked in. Everything was dark and still. He went to the candle-press for a candle, but when he put his hand in the box, the Cat scratched him. He tried to light the candle, but the Dog, dipping his tail in water, shook it and put out the flame. The thief fled. In passing, the White Pet butted him, the Bull kicked him and the Cock began to crow. Outside, the Goose beat her wings about his legs.

He ran to the wood as fast as his legs would carry him.

"What happened?" asked his companions.

"When I went to the candle-press, there was a man in it, and he thrust ten knives into my hand. When I went to the fire to light the candle, there was a big man in the middle of the floor gave me a shove. Another man behind the door pushed me out. There was a little fellow on the loft, calling out: '*Cuir-anees-an-shaw-ay-s-foni-mi-hayn-da! Send him up here, and I'll do for him!*' And there was a shoemaker out on the midden, hitting me about the legs with his apron."

When the thieves heard that, they didn't go back to look for their money. The White Pet and his companions kept it, and they lived happily ever after.

Tam Scott and the Fin-man

[ORKNEY]

TAM SCOTT was at the Lammas Fair in Kirkwall, where he had taken a number of folk from Sanday in his parley boat. He was going up and down through the Fair when he met a tall, dark-faced man.

"The top of the day to you," says the stranger.

"As much to you," says Tam; "but who speaks to me?"

"Never heed," says the man. "Will you take a cow of mine to one of the north isles? I'll pay double freight for taking you so soon from the Fair."

"That I will," says Tam, for he was not the boy to stick at a bargain when he thought the butter was on his side of the bread.

By the time he had got the boat ready, he saw the dark-faced man coming leading his cow. When he came to the edge of the water, the stranger lifted the cow in his arms, as if she had been a sheep, and set her down in the boat.

"Where are we to steer for?" said Tom when they got under way.

"East of Shapinshay," said the man.

"Where now?" said Tam when they reached Shapinshay.

"East of Stronsay," said the man.

Then they reached the Mill Bay of Stronsay.

"You'll be for landing here?" said Tam.

"No, east of Sanday," said the man.

Now, Tam liked a gossip, and as they sailed along he tried to chat to his passenger in a friendly way, but at every remark the stranger only replied gruffly:

"A close tongue keeps a safe head."

At last it began to dawn on Tam's mind that he had an uncanny passenger on board. As they sailed on through the east sea, Tam saw, rising ahead, a dense bank of mist. Soon the bank of mist began to shine like a cloud lit up by the setting sun. Then it began to rise; and Tam saw lying under it a most beautiful island. On that fair land men and women were walking, cattle feeding and yellow cornfields were ripe for the harvest. While Tam was staring with all his eyes at this braw land, the stranger sprang aft.

"I must blindfold you now for a while. If you do what you are told no ill shall befall you," said he.

Tam thought it would only end badly for him if he refused, so he allowed himself to be blindfolded with his own handkerchief. In a few minutes Tam felt the boat grind on a pebbly beach. He heard voices of many men speaking to his passenger, and he also heard the loveliest sound he had ever heard in his life. It was the sweet voices of mermaids singing on the shore. Tam saw them through one corner of his right eye that came below the handkerchief. The braw sight and the bonny sound nearly put him out of his wits for joy. Then he heard a man's voice call:

"You idle creatures, don't think you'll win this man with your singing! He has a wife and bairns of his own in Sanday Isle."

And with that the music changed to a most mournful song. The sound of it made Tam's heart sad indeed.

Well, the cow was soon lifted out, a bag of money laid at Tam's feet in the stern sheets, and the boat shoved off. And what do you think? Those graceless wretches of Fin-men turned his boat against the sun! As they pushed off the boat, one of them cried:

"Keep the starboard end of the fore thraft bearing on the Braes of Warsater, and you'll soon make land."

When Tam felt his boat under way he tore off the bandage, and could see nothing save a thick mist. But he soon sailed out of the mist, and saw it lying astern like a great cloud. Then he saw what pleased him better, the Braes of Warsater bearing on his starboard bow. As he sailed home, he opened his bag of money, and found he had been well paid, but all in coppers. The Fin-folk love the white money too well to part with silver.

Well, in a year Tam went to the Lammas Fair as usual. Many a time afterwards he wished he had lain in his bed that day, but what is to be must be, and cannot be helped.

It happened on the third day of the market, as Tam was walking up and down, speaking to his friends, whom should he see but the same dark-faced man that gave him the freight the year before. In his friendly way Tam went up to the man, and said:

"How is all with you, good man? I am glad to see you this day! Come and take a cog of ale with me. And how have you been since last I saw you?"

"Did you ever see me before?" said the man, with an ugly look on his face.

"I took your cow and yourself in my boat to East of Sanday," said Tam.

"Is that so?" said the man. As he spoke, he took out of his pocket what Tam thought was a snuffbox. Then the man opened the box, and blew some powder out of it right into Tam's eyes, saying:

"Now you will never have to say that you saw me before."

And from that minute poor Tam never again saw a blink of sweet light in his two eyes.

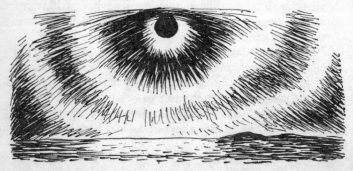

The Legend of Loch Maree

ONCE the King of Denmark sent his son to the Scottish Court. The young Prince took a party of friends with him to hunt, and they landed on the north-west coast of Scotland.

One day, by Loch Maree, the Prince lost his companions, and, feeling tired, sat down and fell asleep.

Awaking, he saw an old man and a young woman coming toward him. Standing in their path, he bowed low.

"Out of my way, stranger!" said the old man.

"I am the Prince of Denmark," said the young man.

The old man made excuses, saying:

"This is the Princess Thyra of Ireland. She is staying with us at the Monastery on Isle Maree, and I have to protect her from intrusion."

"This has been our first meeting and I fear it will be our last," said the Prince to the Princess.

"That may be," she said, and went away with the old man.

The Prince returned, hoping to see her again, but no one came that day. The next time he waited two days. The third time he waited three days, and still no one came. Then he decided to go to Isle Maree.

He found a boatman willing to ferry him across. As they landed on the island, the boatman pointed out a path.

"On your way," he said, "you will come to a Holy Well. You must not pass without drinking from it. Beside the Well is an old oak tree with a hollow side. You should not pass without putting something of value into it."

But the Prince forgot the Holy Well and the hollow tree. He knocked at the door of the Monastery. He was led to an old monk, who asked him who he was, and what he wanted.

"I am the Prince of Denmark," said he, "and I have come to ask the Princess Thyra to marry me."

"The Princess is free to make her own choice," said the old monk.

The Princess was pleased to see him, and they spent the day happily together on the island, but she refused to marry him.

"I saw you only once before," she said. "Love that comes as quickly may go as quickly, and I am afraid. Red Hector of the hills wants to marry me, and he would be a dangerous foe."

"He would meet his match," he said, and went away, promising to return next day.

He had not gone far when an arrow passed close to his face; the next one stuck in his bonnet. A tall man was standing beside a rock.

"Why do you make a target of me?" asked the Prince.

"I am Red Hector of the hills," said the big man. "We have a matter to settle between us. You must kill me or I must kill you!"

"Surely there is a better way to settle our differences," said the Prince.

"There is not," said Red Hector.

So the two men fought. Red Hector struck the Prince with his sword, wounding him deeply.

The Prince lay still and kept his hand on his wound to stop the bleeding. He dragged himself toward a near-by burn, but fainted before he could drink. A monk found him and took him back to the Monastery of Isle Maree. The Princess Thyra nursed him back to life, and promised to go to Denmark with him.

But a ship sailed into Poolewe with bad news. The Princess must return to Ireland, where her father was dying.

"Will you return?" he asked.

"Nothing but death shall prevent me," she replied. So the Princess sailed away.

The Prince's men looked out for her ship from the highest hills. Each day they returned without news.

One day they saw three ships, and the first one had the royal flag of Ireland at its topmast. The Prince took his men to the highest hill to signal a welcome, and on the way they met an old man.

"Wait till I tell you my dream," said he.

"I care nothing for dreams," said the Prince.

"I dreamt this dream three nights," said the old man. "In it the Princess Thyra of Ireland was dead. But I will go to the ship. If all is well, you'll see a red flag flying. If not, a black one."

The old man rowed out to the ship. He persuaded the Princess to fly a black flag, to surprise the Prince when he saw her alive and well.

But when the Prince saw the black flag he took out his dirk and killed himself.

The Princess was told what had happened.

"I will go alone to bid him farewell," she said.

On the way, someone followed her. Turning, she saw the old man.

"Wretched old man!" she cried. "That was evil advice you gave me."

"Old man!" said he, tearing off his disguise. "I am Red Hector of the hills!" With that he killed her with his dirk, and disappeared into the black hills.

Finn and the Grey Dog

[ARGYLLSHIRE]

ONE day Finn and his men were hunting on the hill. They had killed many deer. When they were preparing to go home, they saw a tall lad coming. He greeted Finn, and Finn returned his greeting.

Finn asked him where he came from and what he wanted.

"I have come from the east and from the west, seeking a master," he said.

"I need a lad," said Finn, "and if we can agree, I'll employ you. What reward do you want at the end of a year and a day?"

"Not much," said the lad; "only that you go with me, at the end of the year and the day, to a feast at the palace of the King of Lochlan."

Finn engaged the lad, and he served him faithfully to the end of the year and a day.

On the morning of the last day the tall lad asked Finn if he was satisfied with him. Finn said he was perfectly satisfied.

"Well," said the lad, "I hope I shall have my reward, and that you'll go with me as you promised."

"You'll have your reward," said Finn, "and I'll go with you."

"It is the day I have to keep my promise to the lad," Finn told his men, "and I don't know when I shall return. But if I am not back within a year and a day, let the man who is not whetting his sword be bending his bow to revenge me on the shore of Lochlan!"

When he had said this, he bade them farewell and went into his house. His fool was sitting by the fire.

"Are you sorry I am going away?" Finn asked.

"I am sorry you are going that way," said the fool, weeping, "but I'll give you advice if you'll take it."

"Yes," said Finn, "for often the King's advice has come from the fool's head. What is your advice?"

"It is," said the fool, "to take Bran's chain in your pocket with you."

Finn did so, bade him farewell and went away. He found the tall lad waiting for him at the door.

"Are you ready to go?" said the lad.

"I am ready to go," said Finn. "Lead the way, you know the road better."

The tall lad set off, and Finn followed. Yet, though Finn was swift, he could not touch the tall lad with a stick all the way. When the tall lad was disappearing through a gap in the mountains, Finn would be appearing on the ridge behind him. They kept that distance between them till their journey's end.

They entered the palace of the King of Lochlan, and Finn sat down wearily. But, instead of a feast, the lords of the King of Lochlan were considering how to bring about his death.

"Hang him!" said one. "Burn him!" said another. "Drown him!" said a third.

"Send him to Glenmore!" said another. "He'll not go far there before he's killed by the Grey Dog. There would be no death more disgraceful, in the opinion of the Feinne, than their King's death from a cur."

They all clapped their hands, and agreed with him.

At once they took Finn to the Glen where the Dog was. They had not gone very far up the Glen before they heard the Dog howling. When they saw him, they said it was time to run. So they left Finn at the Dog's mercy.

If Finn ran away, the men would kill him, and if he stayed, the Dog would kill him. He would as soon be killed by the Dog as by his enemies. So he stayed.

The Grey Dog came with his mouth open and his tongue hanging to one side. Every breath from his nostrils burned everything three miles in front of him and on both sides of him. Finn was tortured by the heat, and knew he could not stand it long. If Bran's chain was going to be of any use, now was the time to take it out. He put his hand in his pocket, and when the Dog was near him he took the chain out and shook it. The Dog at once stopped and wagged his tail. He came to Finn, and licked all his sores from head to foot, healing with his tongue what he had burned with his breath. At length Finn put Bran's chain round the Grey Dog's neck and went down the Glen with the Dog on a leash.

An old man and woman, who had fed the Grey Dog, lived at the foot of the Glen. The old woman was at the door, and when she saw Finn coming with the Dog she ran into the house, crying.

"What do you see?" said the old man.

"I saw as tall and handsome a man as ever I saw, coming down the Glen with the Grey Dog on a leash."

"If all the people of Lochlan and Ireland were together," said the old man, "not one man of them could do that, but Finn, King of the Feinne, and Bran's golden chain with him."

"Whether it's he or not, he's coming," replied the old woman.

"We'll soon know," said the old man, going out.

He met Finn, and they greeted each other. Finn told him why he was there, and the old man invited him into the house for rest and a meal. The old woman told Finn he was very welcome to stay for a year and a day, and Finn accepted the invitation.

At the end of the year and a day the old woman was standing on a knowe near the house. She looked toward the shore and saw a great army on the beach of Lochlan. She ran into the house, her eyes big with fear.

"What did you see?" said the old man.

"I saw something I never saw before. There's a great army on the beach, and among them a red-haired man with a squint. I don't think there's his equal, as a fighter, this night under the stars."

"They are my companions," said Finn. "Let me go to meet them."

Finn and the Grey Dog went down to the shore. When his men saw him coming they shouted, so that it was heard in the four corners of Lochlan. They and their King greeted each other, and no less friendly was the greeting between Bran and the Grey Dog, for they were brothers taken together from the castle.

They took vengeance on the men of Lochlan for their treatment of Finn. They began at one end of Lochlan and did not stop till they went out at the other end.

After they had conquered Lochlan they went home, and in the Hall of Finn they made a great feast that lasted a year and a day.

The Smith and the Fairies

[ISLAY]

Years ago there lived in Crossbrig a smith called MacEachern. His only child was a strong, healthy lad about fourteen years old. Suddenly he fell ill, and nobody could tell what was wrong with him. He became thin, old and yellow. His father was afraid he would die, although he had an extraordinary appetite.

One day an old man, well known for his knowledge of out-of-the-way things, walked into the smiddy, and MacEachern told him about the lad.

The old man looked very grave, and said:

"That is not your son. Your lad has been carried away by the fairies, and they have left a changeling in his place."

"What am I to do?" asked the smith. "How am I ever to see my son again?"

"I will tell you how," said the old man. "But first, make sure it is not your own son. Take as many empty egg-shells as you can find. Take them into his room, and spread them

128

out carefully where he can see them. Then fetch water in them, carrying them two by two in your hands as if they were very heavy. When they are full, arrange them round the fire as if it was very important."

The smith did this.

He had not been long at work when there came a shout of crazy laughter from the bed, and a voice said:

"I'm now eight-hundred years old, and I've never seen anything like that before!"

The smith told this to the old man, who said:

"Get rid of this changeling as soon as possible, and I think I can promise you your son. First of all, you must light a very big fire before the changeling's bed. Then you must seize him and throw him into the middle of it, and he will fly through the roof."

The smith took the old man's advice, kindled a large fire, and seizing the changeling, flung him into the fire without hesitation. The changeling gave a terrible yell, and sprang through the roof, leaving a hole that let the smoke out.

Then the old man told him his son was in the green hill of the fairies, and gave him instructions how to find him.

That night the smith took a sleeping cock in his arms, and went out into the darkness. As he drew near the green hill of the fairies he saw a light in it, and heard sounds of piping, dancing and merriment. Boldly the smith approached the entrance and went in. There he saw his own son working at a forge.

The fairies asked him what he wanted.

"I want my son," said he, "and I will not go away without him."

All the fairies laughed loudly. This wakened the cock. It leaped up on his shoulder, clapped its wings, and crowed loud and long. Now, the fairies cannot bear the crowing of a cock, for when they hear it the power of magic leaves them. Mad with anger, the fairies seized the smith and his son and threw them out of the green hill. Instantly all was dark.

For a year and a day the lad did no work, and seldom spoke. One day he was sitting by his father watching him finish a sword for a chief. It was to be a very special sword.

"That is not the way to do it," said his son.

Taking the tools from his father, he set to work, and made a sword the like of which had never before been seen in the country.

From that day the young man worked constantly with his father, and invented a very fine sword. This kept the two men busy, and spread their fame far and wide, so that they became wealthy. And they were never troubled by the fairies again.

Farquhar the Physician

IN the Reay country there was once a drover called
Farquhar. He went from Glen Gollich to England to sell
cattle, and the staff in his hand was of hazel. One day he
met a doctor.

"What's that you have in your hand?" said he.

"It's a hazel staff," said Farquhar.

"Where did you cut it?"

"In Glen Gollich. North in Lord Reay's country," said
he.

"Do you remember the place and the tree?"

"That I do."

"Could you find the tree again?" said the doctor.

"I could," said Farquhar.

"Well, I will give you more gold than you can lift if you
will go back there and bring me a wand off that hazel tree,"
said the doctor.

"I will do that," said Farquhar.

"Take this bottle, and bring me something more, and I
will give you as much gold again," said the doctor. "Watch
at the hole at the foot of the tree, and put a bottle to it. Let
go the six serpents that come out first, but put the seventh in
the bottle. Tell nobody, but come straight back here with
it."

So Farquhar went to Scotland, and the hazel glen, and
when he had cut some boughs off the tree, he looked about
for the hole the doctor had spoken of. He found it, and what
should come out but six serpents, brown and barred like
adders. These he let go, and put the bottle to the hole, to see
if any more would come out. By and by a white snake came
crawling through. In a flash, Farquhar caught it in the

131

bottle. He sealed the bottle and hurried back to England with it.

The doctor gave him gold enough to buy the Reay country.

"Before you return to Scotland," said he, "stay and help me prepare the white snake."

"I will do that," said Farquhar.

They lit a fire with the hazel sticks, and put the white snake into a pot to boil. The doctor had to go away, so he asked Farquhar to watch it, not to let anyone touch it, and not to let the steam escape, for fear folk might know what they were doing.

Farquhar wrapped paper round the pot lid, but he hadn't finished when the water began to boil, and the steam to come out at one place. When he saw this, he decided to push the paper down. He put his finger to the place, and then put his finger, wet with bree, into his mouth.

At once he knew everything, but he decided to tell no one about his knowledge.

When the doctor came back, he took the pot from the fire, lifted the lid, and dipping his finger in the steam drops, sucked it. But it was no more than water to him.

"Who has done this?" he cried, and he saw in Farquhar's face that it was he.

"Since you have taken the bree of it, take the flesh too!" he cried, and, throwing the pot at him, he turned and left him.

Now Farquhar became all-wise. He returned to Scotland, and set up as a physician. There was no secret hid from him, and nothing he could not cure. He went from place to place, healing the sick, so they called him Farquhar the Healer.

One day he heard that the King was sick, and he went to find out what was wrong with him.

"It is in his knee," said all the folk. "He has many doctors, he pays them all well, and sometimes they can give him relief, but not for long. Then it is worse than ever with him, and you can hear him cry out with the pain that is in the bones of his knee."

Farquhar walked up and down before the King's house, crying:

"The black beetle to the white bone!"

The people looked at him and said that the strange man from the Reay country was daft. The next day Farquhar stood at the gate and cried:

"The black beetle to the white bone!"

The King asked who was crying outside, and what was his business. The man, they told him, was a stranger from the Reay country called Farquhar the Physician. So the King, who was wild with pain, called him in. Farquhar stood before the King and said:

"The black beetle to the white bone!"

And so it proved. The doctors, to keep the King ill and to get their fee, at times put a black beetle into the wound in his knee. The creature was eating the bone and the flesh, making him cry out day and night in agony. Then the doctors took it out again, for fear he would die, and as he grew better they put it back again. This Farquhar knew by his serpent's wisdom when he laid his finger under his wisdom tooth. The King was soon cured, and he had all his doctors hung for their wickedness.

The King said he would give Farquhar lands or gold, or whatever he asked. Farquhar asked for the King's daughter, and all the Isles that the sea runs round, from the point of Storr to Stromness in the Orkneys. So the King gave him his daughter, and a grant of all the Isles.

Mally Whuppie
[LOWLAND]

ONCE upon a time there was a man and a wife who had so many children they could not get food for them all. So they took the three youngest and left them in a wood.

The three children walked, and walked, without seeing a house. It began to grow dark, and they were hungry. At last they saw a light, and made for it, and found it was indeed a house.

They knocked at the door. A woman opened it, and asked them what they wanted. They begged her to let them in and give them a bite of bread. The woman said she could not do that, as her husband was a giant, and he would kill them if he came home and found them there.

"Let us remain just for a while," they begged. "We'll go away before your husband returns."

So she took them in and set them down by the fire and gave them bread and milk. But just as they had begun to eat, there was a loud knock on the door.

> *"Fee, fie, fo, fum,*
> *I smell the blood of some earthly one!"*

a terrible voice bellowed. "What have you there, wife?"

"Three poor lasses cold and hungry, and they will go away soon. You won't touch them, husband?"

The giant said nothing, but ate his supper. Then he ordered them to stay all night, and to share a bed with his own three daughters.

Before they went to bed, the giant put straw ropes round the necks of the strangers, while round the necks of his three daughters he put chains of gold. Now, the youngest of the three strangers was called Mally Whuppie. She was very clever, and noticed what the giant had done. She took care not to fall asleep, but waited till she was sure that the others were sound asleep.

Then she slipped out of bed and exchanged the necklaces. The giant's daughters now wore straw necklaces, while Mally Whuppie and her two sisters wore necklaces of gold. She lay down again, pretending to be asleep.

In the middle of the night, up rose the giant, armed with a thick club, and in the dark he felt for the necks with straw ropes. He took his own girls out on the floor, beat them and then lay down again.

Mally Whuppie thought it time she and her sisters were away, so she wakened them and told them to be very quiet. They slipped out of the house, and ran, and ran, till morning, when they came to a King's house.

Mally Whuppie told her story to the King.

"Well, Mally, you are a clever lass," said the King, "and you have done well. But if you would do better, go back and take the giant's sword that hangs on the back of his bed, bring it here to me, and I will give your eldest sister my eldest son to marry."

Mally said that she would try. So she went back, slipped into the giant's house and crept below the bed.

The giant came home, ate a big supper, hung up his sword and went to bed. Mally Whuppie waited until he was snoring, then she crept out, stretched over the giant and took down the sword. But as she did so it gave a rattle, and up jumped the giant. Mally dodged out at the door, the sword with her.

Mally ran, and the giant ran, till they came to the Bridge of One Hair. She won over, but he could not.

"Woe be to you, Mally Whuppie!" cried the giant. "May you never come here again!"

"Twice yet, carle!" said she.

Mally Whuppie took the sword to the King, and her eldest sister was married to his eldest son.

"You've done well, Mally Whuppie," said the King, "but if you can do better, bring me the purse that lies below the giant's pillow, and I will marry your second sister to my second son."

Mally said she would try. So she set out for the giant's house, slipped in below the bed, and waited till the giant had eaten his supper and was snoring.

She crept out, slipped her hand below the pillow and took out the purse. But just as she was going out, the giant awoke, and was after her in no time.

She ran, and he ran, till they came to the Bridge of One Hair. She won over, but he could not.

"Woe betide you, Mally Whuppie," said he. "May you never come here again!"

"Once yet, carle!" said she.

Mally took the purse to the King, and her second sister was married to his second son.

"Mally, you're a clever lass," said the King, "but if you can do better yet, bring me the giant's ring he wears on his finger, and I'll give you my youngest son."

Mally said she would try. So back she went to the giant's house, crept in, hid below the bed and waited till the giant came in and had eaten his supper. Soon he was snoring.

Then Mally crept out, reached over the bed and took hold of the giant's hand. She twisted and twisted till the ring came off. But at that very moment the giant rose and gripped her by the hand.

"Now, I have caught you, Mally Whuppie," said he, "and if I had done as much ill to you as you have done to me, what would you do?"

"I would put you into a bag," said she, "and I would put a cat and a dog beside you, and a needle, thread and shears. Then I would hang you up on the wall. And I would go into the wood for a thick stick, and I would come home and take you down and beat you with it."

"Well, Mally, I'll do just that to you," said the giant.

So he put Mally into a large bag, and the cat and dog in beside her, and a needle, thread and shears. Then he hung her up on the wall, and went to the wood to find a heavy stick."

"Oh, if you saw what I see!" sang Mally, inside the bag.

"What do you see?" asked the giant's wife.

But Mally only went on singing:

"Oh, if you saw what I see!"

The giant's wife begged Mally to take her up into the bag, that she might see what Mally saw. So Mally took the shears and cut a hole in the bag, and jumped out, taking the needle and thread with her. She helped the giant's wife up into the bag, and sewed up the hole.

"I see nothing!" cried the giant's wife. "Let me out!"

But Mally took no notice, and hid herself at the back of the door.

Home came the giant, a great stick in his hand. He took down the bag, and began to beat it.

"Stop! It's me, husband!" cried his wife. "It's me!"

But the dog barked and the cat mewed inside the bag, and he did not hear his wife's voice. Now, Mally did not want the wife to be killed, so she ran out from the back of the door. The giant saw her and was after her.

He ran, and she ran, till they came to the Bridge of One Hair, and she won over, but he could not.

"Woe be to you, Mally Whuppie," he cried. "May you never return here again!"

"Never more, carle," said she.

Mally Whuppie took the ring to the King, and she was married to his youngest son.

The Mermaid

[ARGYLLSHIRE]

ONE day a mermaid rose at the side of a poor fisherman's boat.

"Are you catching many fish?" she asked.

"I am not," said he.

"What will you give me for sending you plenty of fish?"

"Ach," said the old man, "I haven't much to spare."

"Give me your first son," said she.

"I'll give you my son if I have one, but I won't have one now," said he, "my wife is too old."

"What do you have?"

"I have an old mare, an old dog, myself and my old wife. These are all I have in the world."

"Here are twelve grains," said the mermaid. "Give three to your wife, three to your dog, three to your mare, and three you must plant behind your house. In time your wife will have three sons, the mare three foals, and the dog three pups. Three trees will grow behind your house, and when one of your sons dies, one of the trees will wither. Now go home, and remember me when your eldest son is three years of age. You will catch plenty of fish from now on."

Everything happened as the mermaid had said.

At the end of three years he went to fish as usual, but did not take his son with him. The mermaid rose at the side of his boat, and said:

"Have you brought your son to me?"

"I did not bring him. I forgot that this was the day," said he.

"Very well, you may have four more years of him," said the mermaid, and she lifted up her child. "Here is a lad of the same age. Is your son as fine as this one?"

The fisherman went home very happy, for he had four more years. He kept on catching plenty of fish, but at the end of four years he grew sad. He went fishing as before, and the mermaid rose at the side of his boat.

"Have you brought your son to me?" she said.

"I forgot him this time too," said the old man.

"Go home then," said the mermaid, "and seven years from now you are sure to remember me. You'll still catch plenty of fish."

At the end of seven years the old man could rest neither day nor night.

"What is worrying you, Father?" asked his eldest son.

"That is my affair," said the old man.

The lad said he must know, and at last his father told him about the mermaid.

"You shall not go, my son," said he, "though I never catch another fish."

"Then go to the smiddy," said the lad, "and tell him to make me a strong sword, and I'll go seek my fortune."

His father went to the smiddy, and the smith made him a sword. The lad grasped it, and shook it once or twice, and it broke into a thousand pieces. So he asked his father to go to the smiddy and order another sword, twice as heavy. His father did so, and the same thing happened to the next sword.

Back went the old man to the smith, who made the strongest sword, the like of which he had never made before.

"There's a sword for you," said the smith. "The hand must be good that plays this blade."

The old man gave it to his son, who shook it once or twice.

"This will do," said he. "It's high time I was on my way."

The next morning he put a saddle on the black horse, son of the old mare. Away he went, his black dog with him.

When he had gone some way, he saw the carcass of a

sheep beside the road. By the carrion sat a dog, a falcon and an otter. He alighted and divided the carcass among the three.

"If swift foot or sharp tooth will help you, remember me, and I'll be by your side," said the dog.

"If swimming foot at the bottom of a pool will help you, remember me, and I'll be by your side," said the otter.

"If swift wing or crooked claw will help you, remember me, and I'll be by your side," said the falcon.

The lad went on till he reached a King's house, where he took service as a cowherd. He went out with the cattle, but the grass was poor. When evening came, he took them home, but the cows gave little milk, and the lad had little to eat and drink that night.

Next day he took them to a grassy place in a green glen. When he was due to take the cattle home, he saw a giant with a sword in his hand.

"Hiu! Hiu! Hogaraich!" shouted the giant. "My teeth have rotted a long time waiting for you. The cattle are now mine. They are on my land, and you are a dead man!"

"There's no knowing," said the cowherd. "It's easier to say than to do."

Then he called his black dog. With one spring it caught the giant by the neck, and the cowherd struck off his head.

He mounted the black horse, rode to the giant's house, and went in. There was plenty of money, and clothes of silver and gold, but he took nothing.

At the mouth of night he returned to the King's castle. When the cows were milked there was plenty, so he ate well that night. The King was pleased to have such a herd. This went on for some time, but at last all the grass in the glen was eaten.

So he took the cattle farther on till they came to a great park, where he put them. A giant came running.

"Hiu! Hiu! Hogaraich!" shouted the giant. "Your blood shall quench my thirst this night!"

"There's no knowing," said the cowherd.

Then he called his dog. With one spring it caught the giant by the neck, and the cowherd struck off his head.

That night he went home tired, but the cows gave plenty of milk. The King and his family were delighted to have such a herd.

One night the dairymaid was weeping. He asked what was the matter. She said a great beast with three heads was in the loch. It had been given a victim each year, and this year it was the turn of the King's daughter. At midday next day she was to meet the monster at the loch. But a great suitor was going to rescue her.

"What suitor will that be?" said the cowherd.

"He is a great General," said she, "and the King has said that the man who rescues her will marry her."

Next day, near the time, the King's daughter and the General went to meet the beast. They reached the black corrie at the top of the loch. Shortly after, the beast moved in the middle of the loch. But when the General saw the beast with three heads, he hid himself. Then the King's daughter saw a handsome youth, on a black horse, riding toward her. His black dog followed him. He sat down beside her, and told her he had come to rescue her.

"Now I must rest," said he, "and if I fall asleep, you must awaken me as soon as you see the beast."

"How am I to wake you?"

"Put the gold ring from your finger on my little finger."

Not long after she saw the monster coming. She took off her ring and put it on the young man's little finger. He awoke, and went to meet the monster. His black dog sprang on the monster, and the youth was able to cut off one of its heads.

"You have won," said the King's daughter. "I am safe

to-night, but the monster will come again and again, until its other two heads are cut off."

He put a willow twig through the monster's head, and told the King's daughter to bring it back with her next day. She went home with the head over her shoulder, and the cowherd returned to his herding. The General threatened to kill her if she said who had cut off the monster's head.

When they reached the castle, the head was on the General's shoulder. Everyone was very happy that the King's daughter had come home alive.

Next day the General and the King's daughter went back to the loch. When the monster moved in the middle of the loch, the General hid himself, and along came the young man on the black horse with his dog following.

"I'm glad to see you," she said. "Come and rest beside me."

"If I sleep before the beast comes, wake me up," said he.

"How shall I wake you?"

"Take the ear-ring out of your ear, and put it in mine!"

He had just fallen asleep when the King's daughter cried: "Wake up! Wake up!" but wake he would not. But when she took the ear-ring out of her ear, and put it in his, he awoke at once, and went to meet the beast. About the mouth of night he cut another head off the monster. He put the second head on the willow twig, and handed it to the King's daughter. Then he leapt on his black horse, and returned to the herding.

The King's daughter went home with the two heads on the willow twig. The General met her as before, and took them from her.

Everyone was delighted to see her return home alive, and the King was sure that the General would save his daughter.

Next day they returned to the loch, and when the monster moved in the loch, the General hid himself. Along came the lad on the black horse, and lay down beside her.

"If I sleep before the monster comes, wake me," said he.

"How shall I wake you?"

"Take the ear-ring off your other ear, and put it in mine," said he.

No sooner was he asleep than the King's daughter saw the monster.

"Wake up! wake up!" she cried, but wake he would not. So she took the ear-ring from her other ear, and put it in his. He awoke, attacked the beast, and cut off its third head. He put the third head on the willow twig and handed it to the King's daughter. Then he leapt on his horse, and returned to the herding.

The King's daughter went home with the three heads on the willow twig, but the General took them from her.

The King arranged that the General should marry her the next day. But when the priest came, the Princess said she would only marry the man who could take the heads off the twig without cutting it.

"Who should take the heads off the willow twig but the man who put them there?" said the King.

The General tried, but he could not loose them. Then every man in the castle tried, but they could not. There was one other man who had not tried, the cowherd, so he was sent for. He took them off at once.

"The man who cut off the monster's heads has my ring and my ear-rings," said the King's daughter.

The cowherd put his hand in his pocket, and drew out the ring and the ear-rings.

"You are my man," said the Princess.

So they were married that very night.

One day while the Princess and the cowherd were walking by the side of the loch, there came a monster more terrible than the first, and carried him off into the loch.

The Princess met an old smith, and she told him what had happened. The smith told her to spread out all her treasures at the side of the loch. She did so, and the monster put its head out of the water.

"Your jewellery is very fine, Princess," it said.

"Not as fine as the jewel you took from me," said she. "Let me see my husband once, and you shall have anything you see."

The monster brought him.

"Give him to me and you shall have all you see," said she. It did so, threw her husband alive on the shore, and then went away with her jewels.

Soon after this, they were walking beside the loch, when the monster came and took away the Princess. Her husband met the old smith, who told him there was only one way to kill the beast.

"On the island in the middle of the loch is the white-footed hind. Catch her, and out of her will spring a hoodie. Catch the hoodie, and out of her will spring a trout. Catch the trout, and out of it will fall an egg. In the egg is the soul of the monster. Break the egg and the monster will die."

Now the monster sank any boat going to the island, so the cowherd leaped across to the island on his black horse, his black dog after him.

He saw the hind, and the black dog chased her. But when the black dog was on one side of the island the hind was on the other.

"Oh, that the hound I saw by the carcass were here!"

At once the hound was chasing the hind. The two dogs soon brought her to earth. She was no sooner caught than a hoodie sprang out of her.

"Oh, that the grey falcon with the sharp eye and swift wing were here!"

At once the grey falcon was after the hoodie, and brought

her down. She was no sooner caught than a trout sprang out of her into the loch.

"Oh, that the otter were here!"

At once the otter leaped into the loch, and brought the trout back. No sooner was the otter on the shore with the trout than the egg fell from his mouth.

"Don't break the egg," said the monster, "and I'll give you all you ask."

"Give me my wife!" said the cowherd.

At once she was by his side. He took her hand in his, crushed the egg under his foot, and the monster died.

The Prince, who had been a cowherd, was walking with his Princess one day, when he saw a little castle beside a loch in the wood. He asked his wife who lived there. She told him that no one had come back alive who had gone near that castle.

"Things can't be left like that," said he. "I'll find out who is living there."

"Please don't go!" she said.

But he went to the castle, and a little old woman met him at the door.

"Welcome, fisherman's son," said she. "I'm pleased to see you. Come in and rest."

He went in, but she struck him on the back, and he fell dead.

Now, far away in the fisherman's house, they had seen the first tree, planted from the mermaid's grains, withering. The old fisherman's second son said that his elder brother must be dead. He swore he would go and find out where his brother lay. He mounted his black horse, and with his black dog followed his brother's footsteps to the King's castle.

He was so like his elder brother that the King at first thought he was the Princess's husband. Told what had happened, he went to the little castle by the loch and, just as it had happened to the eldest brother, so it happened to him. With one blow the old woman stretched him out dead.

When the fisherman's youngest son saw the second tree withering, he decided to find out how death had come to his two brothers. He mounted his black horse and followed his black dog to the King's castle.

The King was pleased to see him, but at first they would not let him go to the castle by the loch. At last he went, and was met by the old woman.

"Welcome, fisherman's son," said she. "I'm pleased to see you. Come in and rest."

"Go in before me, old woman," said he. "Go in, and let me hear what you have to say."

The old woman went in. He drew his sword and cut off her head. But the sword flew out of his hand. The old woman seized her head with both hands, and stuck it on again. The black dog sprang at her, but she struck the dog a blow with her magic club, and there he lay.

The youngest brother caught the old woman, seized the magic club, and struck her one blow on the top of her head. She fell down dead.

He saw his two brothers lying side by side. He struck each of them with the magic club, and they sprang to their feet. He touched the black dog with it, and up he jumped. They found gold and silver in the old witch's castle, and returned to the King with the treasure.

When the King grew old, the fisherman's eldest son and his wife were crowned King and Queen. They all lived happily ever after.

Cuchulainn and the Two Giants

[ARGYLLSHIRE]

ONCE upon a time there was a King in Scotland whose name was Cumhal. He had a great dog that used to watch the herds. When the cattle were sent out, the dog would lead them to good grass. The dog would herd them there for a day, and in the evening would bring them home.

A man and his wife lived near the King's house, and they had one son. Every evening they sent their son on errands to the King's house.

One evening the boy was going there. He had a ball and a stick, and was playing shinty on the way. The King's dog met him and began to play with the ball, lifting it in his mouth and running with it.

The boy struck the ball in the dog's mouth and drove it down the dog's throat. He choked the dog, and so he had to keep the King's cattle instead of the dog. He drove the cattle to grass in the morning, herded them all day and brought them home in the evening.

So he was called Cuchulainn, which means Cumhal's dog.

One day Cuchulainn was driving the cattle when he saw a giant so big he could see the sky between his legs. The giant came toward him, driving a great ox. The two great horns on the ox had their points backward instead of forward.

"I am going to sleep here," said the giant. "If you see another giant coming, wake me. I will not be easily wakened."

"What is the best way to waken you?" said Cuchulainn.

"Take the biggest stone you can find," said the giant, "and strike me on the chest. That will wake me."

The giant lay and slept. He hadn't slept long when

Cuchulainn saw another giant coming. He was so big he could see the sky between his legs.

Cuchulainn tried to waken the first giant, but waken him he could not. At last he lifted a large stone, and struck the giant on the chest. The giant woke up.

"Is there another giant coming?" said he.

"Yonder he comes," said Cuchulainn, pointing.

"Yes, Crumple Toes, you have stolen my ox," said the other giant.

"I did not steal it, Shamble Shanks," said the first giant.

Shamble Shanks seized one horn of the ox, and Crumple Toes the other. Shamble Shanks broke off his horn at the bone. He threw it away and drove it point foremost into the earth.

He seized the head of the ox, and the two giants hauled. They tore the ox apart, through the middle to the root of the tail. Then they began wrestling.

Cuchulainn started to cut steps at the back of the giant's leg, to make a stair. Shamble Shanks felt something stinging the back of his leg, so he put down his hand and threw Cuchulainn away.

Cuchulainn went feet first into the ox's horn, and could not climb out. Crumple Toes seized his chance, knocked Shamble Shanks down, and killed him. He looked about for Cuchulainn, but could not see him.

"Where are you now, little hero?" said he.

"I am here in the horn," said Cuchulainn.

The giant tried to take him out, but could not put his hand far enough down. At last he straddled his legs, drove his hand into the horn, got hold of Cuchulainn between his two fingers, and brought him up.

Cuchulainn went home with the cattle at the going down of the sun.

Glossary

ain	own.
aloor	alas! alack! (Orkney.)
Assipattle	one who is loath to leave the fireside to do any work. (Orkney.)
bairn	child.
bane	bone.
bannock	oatcake.
ben	mountain.
bicker	bowl or dish.
bide	dwell.
bogle	hobgoblin.
bonnach stone	a stone (usually round) on which bannocks were baked before a fire.
brae	hillside.
braw	handsome, beautiful.
brose	oatmeal or peasemeal mixed with boiling water.
buddo	a term of endearment.
burd	poetic word for woman, lady.
burn	stream.
but	kitchen or outer room.
cannily	cautiously.
carle	man.
clew	a ball of yarn.
cloggirs	goose-grass.
cog, coggie	a wooden vessel for milk, etc.
collop	portion.
corrie	hollow on a mountain side.
creel	basket.
croft	small piece of land adjoining a house.
deil	devil.
dirk	dagger.
doo	dove, pigeon.
Fin-folk	mythical sea folk.
Finn	King of the Feinne.
fulling water	water in which cloth is fulled (milled) and cleansed with soap and fuller's earth.
gien	given.
gillie	man-servant, boy.
girnal	chest for meal, salt, etc.

GLOSSARY

gloaming	twilight.
Gruagach	a kind of brownie with long hair and beard.
haly watter	holy water.
heckle	a comb for dressing flax and hemp.
Hilda-land	Fairy-land.
hoodie	carrion-crow.
Hyn-hallow	Holy Island, between Rousay and Orkney mainland.
ilka	each.
knocking stone	stone-mortar, or flat stone.
knowe	knoll.
laird	squire.
Lammas	the beginning of August.
midden	dunghill.
mind	remember.
mixter-maxter, mixty-maxty	confused, jumbled.
moor-stone	a slab of granite, a standing stone.
Odin stone	a stone sacred to Odin. There is one in Shapinsay.
parley boat	a small boat of a particular rig. See *Stat. Acc.*, xvii. 235.
peerie	small.
St Crispin	saint of shoemakers.
Sassenach	Saxon, foreigner.
selkie	seal.
Sheanachaidh	a reciter of heroic or legendary tales.
shinty	game played with stick and ball in the Highlands.
skirl	a shrill cry.
speyman, speywife	fortune teller.
speir	ask, inquire.
sporran	purse.
stane	stone.
tocher	dowry.
uncanny	ominous, weird.
Uruisg	water hobgoblin.
Warlock	wizard.
waulking	to tread cloth.
whin	gorse.
Whuppity Stoorie	a brownie.
widdershins	counter-clockwise.
yill	ale.

CATCH A KELPIE

If you enjoyed this book
you would probably enjoy our other Kelpies.

Here's a complete list to choose from:

Six Lives Of Fankle The Cat	*George Mackay Brown*
The Magic Walking Stick	*John Buchan*
Sula	*Lavinia Derwent*
Return To Sula	*Lavinia Derwent*
The Desperate Journey	*Kathleen Fidler*
Flash The Sheep Dog	*Kathleen Fidler*
Haki The Shetland Pony	*Kathleen Fidler*
The Story Of Ranald	*Griselda Gifford*
The Spanish Letters	*Mollie Hunter*
The Lothian Run	*Mollie Hunter*
Snake Among The Sunflowers	*Joan Lingard*
Young Barbarians	*Ian Maclaren*
The Hill Of The Red Fox	*Allan Campbell McLean*
Ribbon Of Fire	*Allan Campbell McLean*
A Sound Of Trumpets	*Allan Campbell McLean*
The Well At The World's End	*Norah & William Montgomerie*

MORE FOLK TALES FROM CANONGATE

**FIRESIDE TALES
OF THE TRAVELLER CHILDREN**
Duncan Williamson

SILKIES, BROONIE, AND FAIRIES
Duncan Williamson

RUSSIAN GYPSY TALES
translated by James Riordan

GRIMMS' OTHER TALES
translated and edited by
Ruth Michaelis-Jena & Arthur Ratcliff